Bound to Rise

Horatio Alger

Contents

BOUND TO RISE

BY

Horatio Alger

BIOGRAPHY AND BIBLIOGRAPHY

Horatio Alger, Jr., an author who lived among and for boys and himself remained a boy in heart and association till death, was born at Revere, Mass., January 18, 1884. He was the son of a clergyman; was graduated at Harvard College in 1852, and at its Divinity School in 1860; and was pastor of the Unitarian Church at Brewster, Mass., in 1862-66. In the latter year he settled in New York and began drawing public attention to the condition and needs of street boys. He mingled with them, gained their confidence, showed a personal concern in their affairs, and stimulated them to honest and useful living. With his first story he won the hearts of all red-blooded boys every-where, and of the seventy or more that followed over a million copies were sold during the author's lifetime.

In his later life he was in appearance a short, stout, bald-headed man, with cordial manners and whimsical views of things that amused all who met him. He died at Natick, Mass., July 18, 1899.

Mr. Alger's stories are as popular now as when first published, because they treat of real live boys who were always up and about--just like the boys found everywhere to-day. They are pure in tone and inspiring in influence, and many reforms in the juvenile life of New York may be traced to them. Among the best known are:

Strong and Steady; Strive and Succeed; Try and Trust: Bound to Rise; Risen from the Ranks; Herbert Carter's Legacy; Brave and Bold; Jack's Ward; Shifting for Himself; Wait and Hope; Paul the Peddler; Phil the Fiddler: Slow and Sure: Julius the Street Boy; Tom the Bootblack; Struggling Upward; Facing the World; The Cash Boy; Making His Way; Tony the Tramp; Joe's Luck; Do and Dare: Only an Irish Boy; Sink or Swim; A Cousin's Conspiracy; Andy Gordon; Bob Burton; Harry Vane; Hector's Inheritance; Mark Manson's Triumph; Sam's Chance; The Telegraph Boy; The Young Adventurer; The Young Outlaw; The Young Salesman, and Luke Walton..

CHAPTER I

S it up to the table, children, breakfast's ready."

The speaker was a woman of middle age, not good-looking in the ordinary acceptation of the term, but nevertheless she looked good. She was dressed with extreme plainness, in a cheap calico; but though cheap, the dress was neat. The children she addressed were six in number, varying in age from twelve to four. The oldest, Harry, the hero of the present story, was a broad-shouldered, sturdy boy, with a frank, open face, resolute, though good-natured.

"Father isn't here," said Fanny, the second child.

"He'll be in directly. He went to the store, and he may stop as he comes back to milk."

The table was set in the center of the room, covered with a coarse tablecloth. The breakfast provided was hardly of a kind to tempt an epicure. There was a loaf of bread cut into slices, and a dish of boiled potatoes. There was no butter and no meat, for the family were very poor.

The children sat up to the table and began to eat. They were blessed with good appetites, and did not grumble, as the majority of my readers would have done, at the scanty fare. They had not been accustomed to anything better, and their appetites were not pampered by indulgence.

They had scarcely commenced the meal when the father entered. Like his wife, he was coarsely dressed. In personal appearance he resembled his oldest boy. His wife looking up as he entered perceived that he looked troubled.

"What is the matter, Hiram?" she asked. "You look as if something had happened."

"Nothing has happened yet," he answered; "but I am afraid we are going to lose the cow."

"Going to lose the cow!" repeated Mrs. Walton in dismay.

"She is sick. I don't know what's the matter with her."

"Perhaps it is only a trifle. She may get over it during the day."

"She may, but I'm afraid she won't. Farmer Henderson's cow was taken just that way last fall, and he couldn't save her."

"What are you going to do?"

"I have been to Elihu Perkins, and he's coming over to see what he can do for her. He can save her if anybody can."

The children listened to this conversation, and, young as they were, the elder ones understood the calamity involved in the possible loss of the cow. They had but one, and that was relied upon to furnish milk for the family, and, besides a small amount of butter and cheese, not for home consumption, but for sale at the store in exchange for necessary groceries. The Waltons were too poor to indulge in these luxuries.

The father was a farmer on a small scale; that is, he cultivated ten acres of poor land, out of which he extorted a living for his family, or rather a partial living. Besides this he worked for his neighbors by the day, sometimes as a farm laborer, sometimes at odd jobs of different kinds, for he was a sort of Jack at all trades. But his income, all told, was miserably small, and required the utmost economy and good management on the part of his wife to make it equal to the necessity of a growing family of children.

Hiram Walton was a man of good natural abilities, though of not much education, and after half an hour's conversation with him one would say, unhesitatingly, that he deserved a better fate than his hand-to-hand struggle with poverty. But he was one of those men who, for some unaccountable reason, never get on in the world. They can do a great many things creditably, but do not have the knack of conquering fortune. So Hiram had always been a poor man, and probably always would be poor. He was discontented at times, and often felt the disadvantages of his lot, but he was lacking in energy and ambition, and perhaps this was the chief reason why he did not succeed better.

After breakfast Elihu Perkins, the "cow doctor," came to the door. He was an old man with iron-gray hair, and always wore steel-bowed spectacles; at least for twenty years nobody in the town could remember ever having seen him without them. It was the general opinion that he wore them during the night. Once when questioned on the subject, he laughingly said that he "couldn't see to go to sleep without his specs".

"Well, neighbor Walton, so the cow's sick?" he said, opening the outer door without ceremony.

"Yes, Elihu, she looks down in the mouth. I hope you can save her."

"I kin tell better when I've seen the critter. When you've got through breakfast, we'll go out to the barn."

"I've got through now," said Mr. Walton, whose anxiety for the cow had diminished his appetite.

"May I go too, father?" asked Harry, rising from the table.

"Yes, if you want to."

The three went out to the small, weather-beaten building which served as a barn for the want of a better. It was small, but still large enough to contain all the crops which Mr. Walton could raise. Probably he could have got more out of the land if he had had means to develop its resources; but it was naturally barren, and needed much more manure than he was able to spread over it.

So the yield to an acre was correspondingly small, and likely, from year to year, to grow smaller rather than larger.

They opened the small barn door, which led to the part occupied by the cow's stall. The cow was lying down, breathing with difficulty. Elihu Perkins looked at her sharply through his "specs."

"What do you think of her, neighbor Perkins?" asked the owner, anxiously.

The cow doctor shifted a piece of tobacco from one cheek to the other, and looked wise.

"I think the critter's nigh her end," he said, at last.

"Is she so bad as that?"

"Pears like it. She looks like Farmer Henderson's that died a while ago. I couldn't save her."

"Save my cow, if you can. I don't know what I should do without her."

"I'll do my best, but you mustn't blame me if I can't bring her round. You see there's this about dumb critters that makes 'em harder to cure than human bein's. They can't tell their symptoms, nor how they feel; and that's why it's harder to be a cow doctor than a doctor for humans. You've got to go by the looks, and looks is deceivin'. If I could only ask the critter how she feels, and where she feels worst, I might have some guide to go by. Not but I've had my luck. There's more'n one of 'em I've saved, if I do say it myself."

"I know you can save her if anyone can, Elihu," said Mr. Walton, who appreciated the danger of the cow, and was anxious to have the doctor begin.

"Yes, I guess I know about as much about them critters as anybody," said the garrulous old man, who had a proper appreciation of his dignity and attainments as a cow doctor. "I've had as good success as anyone I know on. If I can't cure her, you may call her a gone case. Have you got any hot water in the house?"

"I'll go in and see."

"I'll go, father," said Harry.

"Well, come right back. We have no time to lose."

Harry appreciated the need of haste as well as his father, and speedily reappeared with a pail of hot water.

"That's right, Harry," said his father. "Now you'd better go into the house and do your chores, so as not to be late for school."

Harry would have liked to remain and watch the steps which were being taken for the recovery of the cow; but he knew he had barely time to do the "chores" referred to before school, and he was far from wishing to be late there. He had an ardent thirst for learning, and, young as he was, ranked first in the district school which he attended. I am not about to present my young hero as a marvel of learning, for he was not so. He had improved what opportunities he had enjoyed, but these were very limited. Since he was nine years of age, his schooling had been for the most part limited to eleven weeks in the year. There was a summer as well as a winter school; but in the summer he only attended irregularly, being needed to work at home. His father could not afford to hire help, and there were many ways in which Harry, though young, could help him. So it happened that Harry, though a tolerably good scholar, was deficient in many respects, on account of the limited nature of his opportunities.

He set to work at once at the chores. First he went to the woodpile and sawed and split a quantity of wood, enough to keep the kitchen stove supplied till he came home again from school in the afternoon. This duty was regularly required of him.

His father never touched the saw or the ax, but placed upon Harry the general charge of the fuel department.

After sawing and splitting what he thought to be sufficient, he carried it into the house by armfuls, and piled it up near the kitchen stove. He next drew several buckets of water from the well, for it was washing day, brought up some vegetables from the cellar to boil for dinner, and then got ready for school.

CHAPTER II
A CALAMITY

Efforts for the recovery of the cow went on. Elihu Perkins exhausted all his science in her behalf. I do not propose to detail his treatment, because I am not sure whether it was the best, and possibly some of my readers might adopt it under similar circumstances, and then blame me for its unfortunate issue. It is enough to say that the cow grew rapidly worse in spite of the hot-water treatment, and about eleven o'clock breathed her last. The sad intelligence was announced by Elihu, who first perceived it.

"The critter's gone," he said. "'Tain't no use doin' anything more."

"The cow's dead!" repeated Mr. Walton, sorrowfully. He had known for an hour that this would be the probable termination of the disease. Still while there was life there was hope. Now both went out together.

"Yes, the critter's dead!" said Elihu, philosophically, for he lost nothing by her. "It was so to be, and there wa'n't no help for it. That's what I thought from the fust, but I was willin' to try."

"Wasn't there anything that could have saved her?"

Elihu shook his head decidedly.

"If she could a-been saved, I could 'ave done it," he said. "What I don't know about cow diseases ain't wuth knowin'."

Everyone is more or less conceited. Elihu's conceit was as to his scientific knowledge on the subject of cows and horses and their diseases. He spoke so confidently that Mr. Walton did not venture to dispute him.

"I s'pose you're right, Elihu," he said; "but it's hard on me."

"Yes, neighbor, it's hard on you, that's a fact. What was she wuth?"

"I wouldn't have taken forty dollars for her yesterday."

"Forty dollars is a good sum."

"It is to me. I haven't got five dollars in the world outside of my farm."

"I wish I could help you, neighbor Walton, but I'm a poor man myself."

"I know you are, Elihu. Somehow it doesn't seem fair that my only cow should be taken, when Squire Green has got ten, and they're all alive and well. If all his cows should die, he could buy as many more and not feel the loss."

"Squire Green's a close man."

"He's mean enough, if he is rich."

"Sometimes the richest are the meanest."

"In his case it is true."

"He could give you a cow just as well as not. If I was as rich as he, I'd do it."

"I believe you would, Elihu; but there's some difference between you and him."

"Maybe the squire would lend you money to buy a cow. He always keeps money to lend on high interest."

Mr. Walton reflected a moment, then said slowly, "I must have a cow, and I don't know of any other way, but I hate to go to him."

"He's the only man that's likely to have money to lend in town."

"Well, I'll go."

"Good luck to you, neighbor Walton."

"I need it enough," said Hiram Walton, soberly. "If it comes, it'll be the first time for a good many years."

"Well, I'll be goin', as I can't do no more good."

Hiram Walton went into the house, and a look at his face told his wife the news he brought before his lips uttered it.

"Is she dead, Hiram?"

"Yes, the cow's dead. Forty dollars clean gone," he said, rather bitterly.

"Don't be discouraged, Hiram. It's bad luck, but worse things might happen."

"Such as what?"

"Why, the house might burn down, or--or some of us might fall sick and die. It's better that it should be the cow."

"You're right there; but though it's pleasant to have so many children round, we shan't like to see them starving."

"They are not starving yet, and please God they won't yet awhile. Some help will come to us."

Mrs. Walton sometimes felt despondent herself, but when she saw her husband affected, like a good wife she assumed cheerfulness, in order to raise his spirits. So now, things looked a little more hopeful to him, after he had talked to his wife. He soon took his hat, and approached the door.

"Where are you going, Hiram?" she asked.

"Going to see if Squire Green will lend me money; enough to buy another cow."

"That's right, Hiram. Don't sit down discouraged, but see what you can do to repair the loss."

"I wish there was anybody else to go to. Squire Green is a very mean man, and he will try to take advantage of any need."

"It is better to have a poor resource than none at all."

"Well, I'll go and see what can be done."

Squire Green was the rich man of the town. He had inherited from his father, just as he came of age, a farm of a hundred and fifty acres, and a few hundred dollars.

The land was not good, and far from productive; but he had scrimped and saved and pinched and denied himself, spending almost nothing, till the little money which the farm annually yielded him had accumulated to a considerable sum. Then, too, as there were no banks near at hand to accommodate borrowers, the squire used to lend money to his poorer neighbors. He took care not to exact more than six per cent. openly, but it was generally understood that the borrower must pay a bonus besides to secure a loan, which, added to the legal interest, gave him a very handsome consideration for the use of his spare funds. So his money rapidly increased, doubling every five or six years through his shrewd mode of management, and every year he grew more economical. His wife had died ten years before. She had worked hard for very poor pay, for the squire's table was proverbially meager, and her bills for dress, judging from her appearance, must have been uncommonly small.

The squire had one son, now in the neighborhood of thirty, but he had not been at home for several years. As soon as he attained his majority he left the homestead, and set out to seek his fortune elsewhere. He vowed he wouldn't any longer submit to the penurious ways of the squire. So the old man was left alone, but he did not feel the solitude. He had his gold, and that was company enough. A time was coming when the two must part company, for when death should come he must leave the gold behind; but he did not like to think of that, putting away the idea as men will unpleasant subjects. This was the man to whom Hiram Walton applied for help in his misfortune.

"Is the squire at home?" he asked, at the back door. In that household the front door was never used. There was a parlor, but it had not been opened since Mrs. Green's funeral.

"He's out to the barn," said Hannah Green, a niece of the old man, who acted as maid of all work.

"I'll go out there."

The barn was a few rods northeast of the house, and thither Mr. Walton directed his steps.

Entering, he found the old man engaged in some light work.

"Good morning, Squire Green."

"Good morning, Mr. Walton," returned the squire.

He was a small man, with a thin figure, and a face deep seamed with wrinkles, more so than might have been expected in a man of his age, for he was only just turned of sixty; but hard work, poor and scanty food and sharp calculation, were responsible for them.

"How are you gettin' on?" asked the squire.

This was rather a favorite question of his, it being so much the custom for his neighbors to apply to him when in difficulties, so that their misfortune he had come to regard as his harvests. .

"I've met with a loss," answered Hiram Walton.

"You don't say so," returned the squire, with instant attention. "What's happened?"

"My cow is dead."

"When did she die?"

"This morning."

"What was the matter?"

"I don't know. I didn't notice but that she was welt enough last night; but this morning when I went out to the barn, she was lying down breathing heavily."

"What did you do?"

"I called in Elihu Perkins, and we worked over her for three hours; but it wasn't of any use; she died half an hour ago."

"I hope it isn't any disease that's catchin'," said the squire in alarm, thinking of his ten. "It would be a bad job if it should get among mine."

"It's a bad job for me, squire. I hadn't but one cow, and she's gone."

"Just so, just so. I s'pose you'll buy another."

"Yes, I must have a cow. My children live on bread and milk mostly. Then there's the butter and cheese, that I trade off at the store for groceries."

"Just so, just so. Come into the house, neighbor Walton."

The squire guessed his visitor's business in advance, and wanted to take time to talk it over. He would first find out how great his neighbor's necessity was, and then he accommodated him, would charge him accordingly.

CHAPTER III
HIRAM'S MOTTO

There was a little room just off the kitchen, where the squire had an old-fashioned desk. Here it was that he transacted his business, and in the desk he kept his papers. It was into this room that he introduced Mr. Walton.

"Set down, set down, neighbor Walton," he said. "We'll talk this thing over. So you've got to have a cow?"

"Yes, I must have one."

The squire fixed his eyes cunningly on his intended victim, and said, "Goin' to buy one in town?"

"I don't know of any that's for sale."

"How much do you calc'late to pay?"

"I suppose I'll have to pay thirty dollars."

Squire Green shook his head.

"More'n that, neighbor Walton. You can't get a decent cow for thirty dollars. I hain't got one that isn't wuth more, though I've got ten in my barn."

"Thirty dollars is all I can afford to pay, squire."

"Take my advice, and get a good cow while you're about it. It don't pay to get a poor one."

"I'm a poor man, squire. I must take what I can get."

"I ain't sure but I've got a cow that will suit you, a red with white spots. She's a fust-rate milker."

"How old is she?"

"She's turned of five."

"How much do you ask for her?"

"Are you going to pay cash down?" asked the squire, half shutting his eyes, and looking into the face of his visitor.

"I can't do that. I'm very short of money."

"So am I," chimed in the squire. He had two hundred dollars in his desk at that moment waiting for profitable investment; but then he didn't call it exactly a lie to misrepresent for a purpose. "So am I. Money's tight, neighbor."

"Money's always tight with me, squire," returned Hiram Walton, with a sigh.

"Was you a-meanin' to pay anything down?" inquired the squire.

"I don't see how I can."

"That alters the case, you know. I might as well keep the cow, as to sell her without the money down."

"I am willing to pay interest on the money."

"Of course that's fair. Wall, neighbor, what do you say to goin' out to see the cow?"

"Is she in the barn?"

"No, she's in the pastur'. 'Tain't fur."

"I'll go along with you."

They made their way by a short cut across a cornfield to the pasture--a large ten-acre lot, covered with a scanty vegetation. The squire's cows could not be said to live in clover.

"That's the critter," he said, pointing out one of the cows which was grazing near by. "Ain't she a beauty?"

"She looks pretty well," said Mr. Walton, dubiously, by no means sure that she would equal his lost cow.

"She's one of the best I've got. I wouldn't sell ef it wasn't to oblige. I ain't at all partic'lar, but I suppose you've got to hev a cow."

"What do you ask for her, squire?"

"She's wuth all of forty dollars," answered the squire, who knew perfectly well that a fair price would be about thirty. But then his neighbor must have a cow, and had no money to pay, and so was at his mercy.

"That seems high," said Hiram.

"She's wuth every cent of it; but I ain't nowise partic'lar about sellin' her."

"Couldn't you say thirty-seven?"

"I couldn't take a dollar less. I'd rather keep her. Maybe I'd take thirty-eight, cash down."

Hiram Walton shook his head.

"I have no cash," he said. "I must buy on credit."

"Wall, then, there's a bargain for you. I'll let you have her for forty dollars, giving you six months to pay it, at reg'lar interest, six per cent. Of course I expect a little bonus for the accommodation."

"I hope you'll be easy with me--I'm a poor man, squire."

"Of course, neighbor; I'm always easy."

"That isn't your reputation," thought Hiram; but he knew that this was a thought to which he must not give expression.

"All I want is a fair price for my time and trouble. We'll say three dollars extra for the accommodation--three dollars down."

Hiram Walton felt that it was a hard bargain the squire was driving with him, but there seemed no help for it.

He must submit to the imposition, or do without a cow. There was no one else to whom he could look for help on any terms. As to the three dollars, his whole available cash amounted to but four dollars, and it was for three quarters of this sum that the squire called. But the sacrifice must be made.

"Well, Squire Green, if that is your lowest price, I suppose I must come to it," he answered, at last.

"You can't do no better," said the squire, with alacrity.

"If so be as you've made up your mind, we'll make out the papers."

"Very well."

"Come back to the house. When do you want to take the cow?"

"I'll drive her along now, if you are willing."

"Why, you see," said the squire, hesitating, while a mean thought entered his mind, "she's been feedin' in my pastur' all the mornin', and I calc'late I'm entitled to the next milkin', you'd better come 'round to-night, just after milkin', and then you can take her."

"I didn't think he was quite so mean," passed through Hiram Walton's mind, and his lip curved slightly in scorn, but he knew that this feeling must be concealed.

"Just as you say," he answered. "I'll come round tonight, or send Harry."

"How old is Harry now?"

"About fourteen."

"He's got to be quite a sizable lad--ought to earn concid'able. Is he industrious?"

"Yes, Harry is a good worker--always ready to lend a hand."

"That's good. Does he go to school?"

"Yes, he's been going to school all the term."

"Seems to me he's old enough to give up larnin' altogether. Don't he know how to read and write and cipher?"

"Yes, he's about the best scholar in school."

"Then, neighbor Walton, take my advice and don't send him any more. You need him at home, and he knows enough to get along in the world."

"I want him to learn as much as he can. I'd like to send him to school till he is sixteen."

"He's had as much schoolin' now as ever I had," said the squire, "and I've got along pooty well. I've been seleckman, and school committy, and filled about every town office, and I never wanted no more schoolin'. My father took me away from school when I was thirteen."

"It wouldn't hurt you if you knew a little more," thought Hiram, who remembered very well the squire's deficiencies when serving on the town school committee.

"I believe in learning," he said. "My father used to say, 'Live and learn.' That's a good motto, to my thinking."

"It may be carried too far. When a boy's got to be of the age of your boy, he'd ought to be thinking of workin.' His time is too valuable to spend in the school-room."

"I can't agree with you, squire. I think no time is better spent than the time that's spent in learning. I wish I could afford to send my boy to college."

"It would cost a mint of money; and wouldn't pay. Better put him to some good business."

That was the way he treated his own son, and for this and other reasons, as soon as he arrived at man's estate, he left home, which had never had any pleasant associations with him. His father wanted to convert him into a money-making machine--a mere drudge, working him hard, and denying him, as long as he could, even the common recreations of boyhood--for the squire had an idea that the time devoted in play was foolishly spent, inasmuch as it brought him in no pecuniary return. He was willfully blind to the faults and defects of his system, and their utter failure in the case of his own son, and would, if could, have all the boys in town brought up after severely practical method. But, fortunately for Harry, Mr. Walton had very different notions. He was compelled to keep his son home the greater part of the summer, but it was against his desire.

"No wonder he's a poor man," thought the squire, after his visitor returned home. "He ain't got no practical idees. Live and learn! that's all nonsense. His boy looks strong and able to work, and it's foolish sendin' him school any longer. That wa'n't my way, and see where I am," he concluded, with complacent remembrance of bonds and mortgages and money out at interest. "That was a pooty good cow trade," he concluded. "I didn't calc' late for to get more'n thirty-five dollars for the critter; but then neighbor Walton had to have a cow, and had to pay my price."

Now for Hiram Walton's reflections.

"I'm a poor man," he said to himself, as he walked slowly homeward, "but I wouldn't be as mean as Tom Green for all the money he's worth. He's made a hard bargain with me, but there was no help for it."

CHAPTER IV
A SUM IN ARITHMETIC

Harry kept on his way to school, and arrived just the bell rang. Many of my readers have seen a country schoolhouse, and will not be surprised to learn that the one in which our hero obtained his education was far from stately or ornamental, architecturally speaking. It was a one-story structure, about thirty feet square, showing traces of having been painted once, but standing greatly in need of another coat. Within were sixty desks, ranged in pairs, with aisles running between them. On one side sat the girls, on the other the boys. These were of all ages from five to sixteen. The boys' desks had suffered bad usage, having been whittled and hacked, and marked with the initials of the temporary occupants, with scarcely an exception. I never knew a Yankee boy who was not the possessor of a knife of some kind, nor one who could resist the temptation of using it for such unlawful purposes. Even our hero shared the common weakness, and his desk was distinguished from the rest by "H. W." rudely carved in a conspicuous place.

The teacher of the school for the present session was Nathan Burbank, a country teacher of good repute, who usually taught six months in a year, and devoted the balance of the year to surveying land, whenever he could get employment in that line, and the cultivation of half a dozen acres of land, which kept him in vegetables, and enabled him to keep a cow. Altogether he succeeded in making a fair living, though his entire income would seem very small to many of my readers. He was not deeply learned, but his education was sufficient to meet the limited requirements of a country school.

This was the summer term, and it is the usual custom in New England that the summer schools should be taught by females. But in this particular school the experiment had been tried, and didn't work. It was found that the scholars were too unruly to be kept in subjection by a woman, and the school committee had therefore engaged Mr. Burbank, though, by so doing, the school term was shortened, as he asked fifty per cent. higher wages than a female teacher would have done. However, it was better to have a short school than an unruly school, and so the district acquiesced.

Eight weeks had not yet passed since the term commenced, and yet this was the last day but one. To-morrow would be examination day. To this Mr. Burbank made reference in a few remarks which he made at the commencement of the exercises.

He was rather a tall, spare man, and had a habit of brushing his hair upward, thus making the most of a moderate forehead. Probably he thought it made him look more intellectual.

"Boys and girls," he said, "to-morrow is our examination day. I've tried to bring you along as far as possible toward the temple of learning, but some of you have held back, and have not done as well as I should like--John Plympton, if you don't stop whispering I'll keep you after school--I want you all to remember that knowledge is better than land or gold. What would you think of a man who was worth a great fortune, and couldn't spell his name?--Mary Jones, can't you sit still till I get through?--It will be well for you to improve your opportunities while you are young, for by and by you will grow up, and have families to support, and will have no chance to learn--Jane Quimby, I wish you would stop giggling, I see nothing to laugh at--There are some of you who have studied well this term, and done the best you could. At the beginning of the term I determined to give a book to the most deserving scholar at the end of the term. I have picked out the boy, who, in my opinion, deserves it--Ephraim Higgins, you needn't move round in your seat. You are not the one."

There was a general laugh here, for Ephraim was distinguished chiefly for his laziness.

The teacher proceeded:

"I do not mean to tell you to-day who it is. To-morrow I shall call out his name before the school committee, and present him the prize. I want you to do as well as you can to-morrow. I want you to do yourselves credit, and to do me credit, for I do not want to be ashamed of you. Peter Shelby, put back that knife into your pocket, and keep it there till I call up the class in whittling."

There was another laugh here at the teacher's joke, and Peter himself displayed a broad grin on his large, good-humored face.

"We will now proceed to the regular lessons," said Mr. Burbank, in conclusion. "First class in arithmetic will take their places."

The first class ranked as the highest class, and in it was Harry Walton.

"What was your lesson to-day?" asked the teacher.

"Square root," answered Harry.

"I will give you out a very simple sum to begin with. Now, attention all! Find the square root of 625. Whoever gets the answer first may hold up his hand."

The first to hold up his hand was Ephraim Higgins.

"Have you got the answer?" asked Mr. Burbank in some surprise. "Yes, sir."

"State it."

"Forty-five."

"How did you get it?"

Ephraim scratched his head, and looked confused. The fact was, he was entirely ignorant of the method of extracting the square root, but had slyly looked at the slate of his neighbor, Harry Walton, and mistaken the 25 for 45, and hurriedly announced the answer, in the hope of obtaining credit for the same.

"How did you get it?" asked the teacher again.

Ephraim looked foolish.

"Bring me your slate."

Ephraim reluctantly left his place, and went up to Mr. Burbank.

"What have we here?" said the teacher. "Why, you have got down the 625, and nothing else, except 45. Where did you get that answer?"

"I guessed at it," answered Ephraim, hard pressed for an answer, and not liking to confess the truth--namely, that he had copied from Harry Walton.

"So I supposed. The next time you'd better guess a little nearer right, or else give up guessing altogether. Harry Walton, I see your hand up. What is your answer?"

"Twenty-five, sir."

"That is right."

Ephraim looked up suddenly. He now saw the explanation of his mistake.

"Will you explain how you did it? You may go to the blackboard, and perform the operation once more, explaining as you go along, for the benefit of Ephraim Higgins, and any others who guessed at the answer. Ephraim, I want you to give particular attention, so that you can do yourself more credit next time. Now Harry, proceed."

Our hero explained the sum in a plain, straightforward way, for he thoroughly understood it.

"Very well," said the schoolmaster, for this, rather than teacher, is the country name of the office. "Now, Ephraim, do you think you can explain it?"

"I don't know, sir," said Ephraim, dubiously.

"Suppose you try. You may take the same sum."

Ephraim advanced to the board with reluctance, for he was not ambitious, and had strong doubts about his competence for the task.

"Put down 625."

Ephraim did so.

"Now extract the square root. What do you do first?"

"Divide it into two figures each."

"Divide it into periods of two figures each, I suppose you mean. Well, what will be the first period?"

"Sixty-two," answered Ephraim.

"And what will be the second?"

"I don't see but one other figure."

"Nor I. You have made a mistake. Harry, show to point it off."

Harry Walton did so.

"Now what do you do next?"

"Divide the first figure by three."

"What do you do that for?"

Ephraim didn't know. It was only a guess of his, because he knew that the first figure of the answer was two, and this would result from dividing the first figure by three.

"To bring the answer," he replied.

"And I suppose you divide the next period by five, for the same reason, don't you?"

"Yes, sir."

"You may take your seat, sir. You are an ornament to the class, and you may become a great mathematician, if you live to the age of Methuselah. I rather think it will take about nine hundred years for you to reach that, point."

The boys laughed. They always relish a joke at the expense of a companion, especially when perpetrated by the teacher.

"Your method of extracting the square root is very original. You didn't find it in any arithmetic, did you?"

"No, sir."

"So I thought. You'd better take out a patent for it. The next boy may go to the board."

I have given a specimen of Mr. Burbank's method of conducting the school, but do not propose to enter into further details at present. It will doubtless recall to some of my readers experiences of their own, as the school I am describing is very similar to hundreds of country schools now in existence, and Mr. Burbank is the representative of a large class.

CHAPTER V
THE PRIZE WINNER

A re you going to the examination to-day, mother?" asked Harry, at breakfast.

"I should like to go," said Mrs. Walton, "but I don't see how I can. To-day's my bakin' day, and somehow my work has got behindhand during the week."

"I think Harry'll get the prize," said Tom, a boy of ten, not heretofore mentioned. He also attended the school, but was not as promising as his oldest brother.

"What prize?" asked Mrs. Walton, looking up with interest.

"The master offered a prize, at the beginning of the term, to the scholar that was most faithful to his studies."

"What is the prize?"

"A book."

"Do you think you will get it, Harry?" asked his mother.

"I don't know," said Harry, modestly. "I think I have some chance of getting it."

"When will it be given?"

"Toward the close of the afternoon."

"Maybe I can get time to come in then; I'll try."

"I wish you would come, mother," said Harry earnestly. "Only don't be disappointed if I don't get it. I've been trying, but there are some other good scholars."

"You're the best, Harry," said Tom.

"I don't know about that. I shan't count my chickens before they are hatched. Only if I am to get the prize I should like to have mother there."

"I know you're a good scholar, and have improved your time," said Mrs. Walton. "I wish your father was rich enough to send you to college."

"I should like that very much," said Harry, his eyes sparkling at merely the suggestion.

"But it isn't much use hoping," continued his mother, with a sigh. "It doesn't seem clear whether we can get a decent living, much less send our boy to college. The cow is a great loss to us."

Just then Mr. Walton came in from the barn.

"How do you like the new cow, father?" asked Harry.

"She isn't equal to our old one. She doesn't give as much milk within two quarts, if this morning's milking is a fair sample."

"You paid enough for her," said Mrs. Walton.

"I paid too much for her," answered her husband, "but it was the best I could do. I had to buy on credit, and Squire Green knew I must pay his price, or go without."

"Forty-three dollars is a great deal of money to pay for a cow."

"Not for some cows. Some are worth more; but this one isn't."

"What do you think she is really worth?"

"Thirty-three dollars is the most I would give if I had the cash to pay."

"I think it's mean in Squire Green to take such advantage of you," said Harry.

"You mustn't say so, Harry, for it won't do for me to get the squire's ill will. I am owing him money. I've agreed to pay for the cow in six months."

"Can you do it?"

"I don't see how; but the money's on interest, and it maybe the squire'll let it stay. I forgot to say, though, that last evening when I went to get the cow he made me agree to forfeit ten dollars if I was not ready with the money and interest in six months. I am afraid he will insist on that if I can't keep my agreement."

"It will be better for you to pay, and have done with it."

"Of course. I shall try to do it, if I have to borrow the money. I suppose I shall have to do that."

Meantime Harry was busy thinking. "Wouldn't it be possible for me to earn money enough to pay for the cow in six months? I wish I could do it, and relieve father."

He began to think over all the possible ways of earning money, but there was nothing in particular to do in the town except to work for the farmers, and there was very little money to earn ill that way. Money is a scarce commodity with farmers everywhere. Most of their income is in the shape of farm produce, and used in the family. Only a small surplus is converted into money, and a dollar, therefore, seems more to them than to a mechanic, whose substantial income is perhaps less. This is the reason, probably, why farmers are generally loath to spend money. Harry knew that if he should hire out to a farmer for the six months the utmost he could expect would be a dollar a week, and it was not certain he could earn that. Besides, he would probably be worth as much to his father as anyone, and his labor in neither case provide money to pay for the cow. Obviously that would not answer. He must think of some other way, but at present none seemed open. He sensibly deferred thinking till after the examination.

"Are you going to the school examination, father?" asked our hero.

"I can't spare time, Harry. I should like to, for I want to know how far you have progressed. 'Live and learn,' my boy. That's a good motto, though Squire Green thinks that 'Live and earn' is a better."

"That's the rule he acts on," said Mrs. Walton. "He isn't troubled with learning."

"No, he isn't as good a scholar probably as Tom, here."

"Isn't he?" said Tom, rather complacently.

"Don't feel too much flattered, Tom," said his mother.

"You don't know enough to hurt you."

"He never will," said his sister, Jane, laughing.

"I don't want to know enough to hurt me," returned Tom, good humoredly. He was rather used to such compliments, and didn't mind them.

"No," said Mr. Walton; "I am afraid I can't spare time to come to the examination. Are you going, mother?"

It is quite common in the country for husbands to address wives in this manner.

"I shall try to go in the last of the afternoon," said Mrs. Walton.

"If you will come, mother," said Harry, "we'll all help you afterwards, so you won't lose anything by it."

"I think I will contrive to come."

The examination took place in the afternoon. Mr. Burbank preferred to have it so, for two reasons. It allowed time to submit the pupils to a previous private examination in the morning, thus insuring a better appearance in the afternoon. Besides, in the second place, the parents were more likely to be at liberty to attend in the afternoon, and he naturally liked to have as many visitors as possible. He was really a good teacher, though his qualifications were limited; but as far as his knowledge went, he was quite successful in imparting it to others.

In the afternoon there was quite a fair attendance of parents and friends of the scholars, though some did not come in till late, like Mrs. Walton. It is not my intention to speak of the examination in detail. My readers know too little of the scholars to make that interesting. Ephraim Higgins made some amusing mistakes, but that didn't excite any surprise, for his scholarship was correctly estimated in the village. Tom Walton did passably well, but was not likely to make his parents proud of his performances. Harry, however, eclipsed himself. His ambition had been stirred by the offer of a prize, and he was resolved to deserve it. His recitations were prompt and correct, and his answers were given with confidence. But perhaps he did himself most credit in declamation. He had always been very fond of that, and though he had never received and scientific instruction in it, he possessed a natural grace and a deep feeling of earnestness which made success easy. He had selected an extract from Webster--the reply to the Hayne--and this was the showpiece of the afternoon. The rest of the declamation was crude enough, but Harry's impressed even the most ignorant of his listeners as superior for a boy of his age. When he uttered his last sentence, and made a parting bow, there was subdued applause, and brought a flush of gratification to the cheek of our young hero.

"This is the last exercise," said the teacher "except one. At the commencement of the term, I offered a prize to the scholar that would do the best from that time till the close of the school. I will now award the prize. Harry Walton, come forward."

Harry rose from his seat, his cheeks flushed again with gratification, and advanced to where the teacher was standing.

"Harry," said Mr. Burbank, "I have no hesitation in giving you the prize. You have excelled all the other scholars, and it is fairly yours. The book is not of much value, but I think you will find it interesting and instructive. It is the life of the great American philosopher and statesman, Benjamin Franklin. I hope you will read and profit by it, and try like him to make your life a credit to yourself and a blessing to mankind."

"Thank you, sir," said Harry, bowing low. "I will try to do so."

There was a speech by the chairman of the school committee, in which allusion was made to Harry and the prize, and the exercises were over. Harry received the congratulations of his schoolmates and others with modest satisfaction, but he was most pleased by the evident pride and pleasure which his mother exhibited, when she, too, was congratulated on his success. His worldly prospects were very uncertain, but he had achieved the success for which he had been laboring, and he was happy.

Chapter VI
LOOKING OUT ON THE WORLD

It was not until evening that Harry had a chance to look at his prize. It was a cheap book, costing probably not over a dollar; but except his schoolbooks, and a ragged copy of "Robinson Crusoe," it was the only book that our hero possessed. His father found it difficult enough to buy him the necessary books for use in school, and could not afford to buy any less necessary. So our young hero, who was found of reading, though seldom able to gratify his taste, looked forward with great joy to the pleasure of reading his new book. He did not know much about Benjamin Franklin, but had a vague idea that he was a great man.

After his evening "chores" were done, he sat down by the table on which was burning a solitary tallow candle, and began to read. His mother was darning stockings, and his father had gone to the village store on an errand.

So he began the story, and the more he read the more interesting he found it. Great as he afterwards became, he was surprised to find that Franklin was a poor boy, and had to work for a living. He started out in life on his own account, and through industry, frugality, perseverance, and a fixed determination to rise in life, he became a distinguished an in the end, and a wise man also, though his early opportunities were very limited. It seemed to Harry that there was a great similarity between his own circumstances and position in life and those of the great man about whom he was reading, and this made the biography the more fascinating. The hope came to him that, by following Franklin's example, he, too, might become a successful man.

His mother, looking up at intervals from the stockings which had been so repeatedly darned that the original texture was almost wholly lost of sight of, noticed how absorbed he was.

"Is your book interesting, Harry?" she asked.

"It's the most interesting book I ever read," said Harry, with a sigh of intense enjoyment.

"It's about Benjamin Franklin, isn't it?"

"Yes. Do you know, mother, he was a poor boy, and he worked his way up?"

"Yes, I have heard so, but I never read his life."

"You'd better read this when I have finished it. I've been thinking that there's a chance for me, mother."

"A chance to do what?"

"A chance to be somebody when I get bigger. I'm poor now, but so was Franklin. He worked hard, and tried to learn all he could. That's the way he succeeded. I'm going to do the same."

"We can't all be Franklins, my son," said Mrs. Walton, not wishing her son to form high hopes which might be disappointed in the end.

"I know that, mother, and I don't expect to be a great man like him. But if I try hard I think I can rise in the world, and be worth a little money."

"I hope you wont' be as poor as your father, Harry," said Mrs. Walton, sighing, as she thought of the years of pain privation and pinching poverty reaching back to the time of their marriage. They had got through it somehow, but she hoped that their children would have a brighter lot.

"I hope not," said Harry. "If I ever get rich, you shan't have to work any more."

Mrs. Walton smiled faintly. She was not hopeful, and thought it probable that before Harry became rich, both she and her husband would be resting from their labor in the village churchyard. But she would not dampen Harry's youthful enthusiasm by the utterance of such a thought.

"I am sure you won't let your father and mother want, if you have the means to prevent it," she said aloud.

"We can't any of us tell what's coming, but I hope you may be well off some time."

"I read in the country paper the other day that many of the richest men in Boston and New York were once poor boys," said Harry, in a hopeful tone.

"So I have heard," said his mother.

"If they succeeded I don't see why I can't."

"You must try to be something more than a rich man. I shouldn't want you to be like Squire Green."

"He is rich, but he is mean and ignorant. I don't think I shall be like him. He has cheated father about the cow."

"Yes, he drove a sharp trade with him, taking advantage of his necessities. I am afraid your father won't be able to pay for the cow six months from now."

"I am afraid so, too."

"I don't see how we can possibly save up forty dollars. We are economical now as we can be."

"That is what I have been thinking of, mother. There is no chance of father's paying the money."

"Then it won't be paid, and we shall be worse off when the note comes due, than now."

"Do you think," said Harry, laying down the book on the table, and looking up earnestly, "do you think, mother, I could any way earn the forty dollars before it is to be paid?"

"You, Harry?" repeated his mother, in surprise, "what could you do to earn the money?"

"I don't know, yet," answered Harry; "but there are a great many things to be done."

"I don't know what you can do, except to hire out to a farmer, and they pay very little. Besides, I don't know of any farmer in the town that wants a boy. Most of them have boys of their own, or men."

"I wasn't thinking of that," said Harry. "There isn't much chance there."

"I don't know of any work to do here."

"Nor I, mother. But I wasn't thinking of staying in town."

"Not thinking of staying in town!" repeated Mrs. Walton, in surprise. "You don't want to leave home, do you?"

"No, mother, I don't want to leave home, or I wouldn't want to, if there was anything to do here. But you know there isn't. Farm work wont' help me along, and I don't' like it as well as some other kinds of work. I must leave home if I want to rise in the world."

"But your are too young, Harry."

This was touching Harry on a tender spot. No boy of fourteen likes to be considered very young. By that time he generally begins to feel a degree of self-confidence and self-reliance, and fancies he is almost on the threshold of manhood. I know boys of fourteen who look in the glass daily for signs of a coming mustache, and fancy they can see plainly what is not yet visible. Harry had not got as far as that, but he no longer looked upon himself as a young boy. He was stout and strong, and of very good height for his age, and began to feel manly. So he drew himself up, upon this remark of his mother's, and said proudly: "I am going on fifteen"--that sounds older than fourteen--"and I don't call that very young."

"It seems but a little while since you were a baby," said his mother, meditatively.

"I hope you don't think me anything like a baby now, mother," said Harry, straightening up, and looking as large as possible.

"No, you're quite a large boy, now. How quick the years have passed!"

"And I am strong for my age, too, mother. I am sure I am old enough to take care of myself."

"But you are young to go out into the world."

"I don't believe Franklin was much older than I, and he got along. There are plenty of boys who leave home before they are as old as I am."

"Suppose you are sick, Harry?"

"If I am I'll come home. But you know I am very healthy, mother, and if I am away from home I shall be very careful."

"But you would not be sure of getting anything to do."

"I'll risk that, mother," said Harry, in a confident tone.

"Did you think of this before you read that book?"

"Yes, I've been thinking of it for about a month; but the book put it into my head to-night. I seem to see my way clearer than I did. I want most of all, to earn money enough to pay for the cow in six months. You know yourself, mother, there isn't any chance of father doing it himself, and I can't earn anything if I stay at home."

"Have you mentioned the matter to your father yet, Harry?"

"No, I haven't. I wish you would speak about it tonight, mother. You can tell him first what makes me want to go."

"I'll tell him that you want to go; but I won't promise to say I think it a good plan."

"Just mention it, mother, and then I'll talk with him about it to-morrow."

To this Mrs. Walton agreed, and Harry, after reading a few pages more in the "Life of Franklin," went up to bed; but it was some time before he slept. His mind was full of the new scheme on which he had set his heart.

CHAPTER VII
IN FRANKLIN'S FOOTSTEPS

Father," said Harry, the next morning, as Mr. Walton was about to leave the house, "there's something I want to say to you."

"What is it?" asked his father, imagining it was some trifle.

"I'll go out with you, and tell you outside."

"Very well, my son."

Harry put on his cap, and followed his father into the open air.

"Now, my son, what is it?"

"I want to go away from home."

"Away from home! Where?" asked Mr. Walton, in surprise.

"I don't know where; but somewhere where I can earn my own living."

"But you can do that here. You can give me your help on the farm, as you always have done."

"I don't like farming, father."

"You never told me that before. Is it because of the hard work?"

"No," said Harry, earnestly. "I am not afraid of hard work; but you know how it is, father. This isn't a very good farm, and it's all you can do to make a living for the rest of us out of it. If I could go somewhere, where I could work at something else, I could send you home my wages."

"I am afraid a boy like you couldn't earn very large wages."

"I don't see why not, father. I'm strong and stout, and willing to work."

"People don't give much for boys' work."

"I don't expect much; but I know I can get something, and by and by it will lead to more. I want to help you to pay for that cow you've just bought of Squire Green."

"I don't see how I'm going to pay for it," said Mr. Walton, with a sigh. "Hard money's pretty scarce, and we farmers don't get much of it."

"That's just what I'm saying, father. There isn't much money to be got in farming. That's why I want to try something else."

"How long have you been thinking of this plan, Harry?"

"Only since last night."

"What put it into your head?"

"That book I got as a prize."

"It is the life of Franklin, isn't it?"

"Yes."

"Did he go away from home when he was a boy?"

"Yes, and he succeeded, too."

"I know he did. He became a famous man. But it isn't every boy that is like Franklin."

"I know that. I never expect to become a great man like him; but I can make something."

Harry spoke those words in a firm, resolute tone, which seemed to indicate a consciousness of power. Looking in his son's face, the elder Walton, though by no means a sanguine man, was inclined to think favorably of the scheme, But he was cautious, and he did not want Harry to be too confident of success.

"It's a new idea to me," he said. "Suppose you fail?"

"I don't mean to."

"But suppose you do--suppose you get sick?"

"Then I'll come home. But I want to try. There must be something for me to do in the world."

"There's another thing, Harry. It takes money to travel round, and I haven't got any means to give you."

"I don't want any, father. I mean to work my way. I've got twenty-five cents to start with. Now, father, what do you say?"

"I'll speak to your mother about it."

"To-day?"

"Yes, as soon as I go in."

With this Harry was content. He had a good deal of confidence that he could carry his point with both parents. He went into the house, and said to his mother:

"Mother, father's going to speak to you about my going away from home. Now don't you oppose it."

"Do you really think it would be a good plan, Harry?"

"Yes, mother."

"And if you're sick will you promise to come right home?"

"Yes, I'll promise that."

"Then I won't oppose your notion, though I ain't clear about its being wise."

"We'll talk about that in a few months, mother."

"Has Harry spoken to you about his plan of going away from home?" asked the farmer, when he reentered the house.

"Yes," said Mrs. Walton.

"What do you think?"

"Perhaps we'd better let the lad have his way. He's promised to come home if he's taken sick."

"So let it be, then, Harry. When do you want to go?"

"As soon as I can."

"You'll have to wait till Monday. It'll take a day or two to fix up your clothes," said his mother.

"All right, mother."

"I don't know but you ought to have some new shirts. You haven't got but two except the one you have on."

"I can get along, mother. Father hasn't got any money to spend for me. By the time I want some new shirts, I'll buy them myself."

"Where do you think of going, Harry? Have you any idea?"

"No, mother. I'm going to trust to luck. I shan't go very far. When I've got fixed anywhere I'll write, and let you know."

In the evening Harry resumed the "Life of Franklin," and before he was ready to go to bed he had got two thirds through with it. It possessed for him a singular fascination. To Harry it was no alone the "Life of Benjamin Franklin." It was the chart by which he meant to steer in the unknown career which stretched before him. He knew so little of the world that he trusted implicitly to that as a guide, and he silently stored away the wise precepts in conformity with which the great practical philosopher had shaped and molded his life.

During that evening, however, another chance was offered to Harry, as I shall now describe.

As the family were sitting around the kitchen table, on which was placed the humble tallow candle by which the room was lighted, there was heard a scraping at the door, and presently a knock. Mr. Walton answered it in person, and admitted the thin figure and sharp, calculating face of Squire Green.

"How are you, neighbor?" he said, looking about him with his parrotlike glance. "I thought I'd just run in a minute to see you as I was goin' by."

"Sit down, Squire Green. Take the rocking-chair."

"Thank you, neighbor. How's the cow a-doin'?"

"Middling well. She don't give as much milk as the one I lost."

"She'll do better bymeby. She's a good bargain to you, neighbor."

"I don't know," said Hiram Walton, dubiously. "She ought to be a good cow for the price you asked."

"And she is a good cow," said the squire, emphatically; "and you're lucky to get her so cheap, buyin' on time. What are you doin' there, Harry? School through, ain't it?"

"Yes, sir."

"I hear you're a good scholar. Got the prize, didn't you?"

"Yes," said Mr. Walton; "Harry was always good at his books."

"I guess he knows enough now. You'd ought to set him to work."

"He is ready enough to work," said Mr. Walton. "He never was lazy."

"That's good. There's a sight of lazy, shiftless boys about in these days. Seems as if they expected to earn their bread 'n butter a-doin' nothin'. I've been a thinkin', neighbor Walton, that you'll find it hard to pay for that cow in six months."

"I am afraid I shall," said the farmer, thinking in surprise, "Can he be going to reduce the price?"

"So I thought mebbe we might make an arrangement to make it easier."

"I should be glad to have it made easier, squire. It was hard on me, losing that cow by disease."

"Of course. Well, what I was thinkin' was, you might hire out your boy to work for me. I'd allow him two dollars a month and board, and the wages would help pay for the cow."

Harry looked up in dismay at this proposition. He knew very well the meanness of the board which the squire provided, how inferior it was even to the scanty, but well-cooked meals which he got at home; he knew, also that the squire had the knack of getting more work out of his men than any other farmer in the town; and the prospect of being six months in his employ was enough to terrify him. He looked from Squire Green's mean, crafty face to his father's in anxiety and apprehension. Were all his bright dreams of future success to terminate in this?

CHAPTER VIII
HARRY'S DECISION

Squire Green rubbed his hands as if he had been proposing a plan with special reference to the interest of the Waltons. Really he conceived that it would save him a considerable sum of money. He had in his employ a young man of eighteen, named Abner Kimball, to whom he was compelled to pay ten dollars a month. Harry, he reckoned, could be made to do about as much, though on account of his youth he had offered him but two dollars, and that not to be paid in cash.

Mr. Walton paused before replying to his proposal.

"You're a little too late," he said, at last, to Harry's great relief.

"Too late!" repeated the squire, hastily. "Why, you hain't hired out your boy to anybody else, have you?"

"No; but he has asked me to let him leave home, and I've agreed to it."

"Leave home? Where's he goin'?"

"He has not fully decided. He wants to go out and seek his fortune."

"He'll fetch up at the poorhouse," growled the squire.

"If he does not succeed, he will come home again."

"It's a foolish plan, neighbor Walton. Take my word for't. You'd better keep him here, and let him work for me."

"If he stayed at home, I should find work for him on my farm."

Mr. Walton would not have been willing to have Harry work for the squire, knowing well his meanness, and how poorly he paid his hired men.

"I wanted to help you pay for that cow," said the squire, crossly. "If you can't pay for't when the time comes you mustn't blame me."

"I shall blame no one. I can't foresee the future; but I hope to get together the money somehow."

"You mustn't ask for more time. Six months is a long time to give."

"I believe I haven't said anything about more time yet, Squire Green," said Hiram Walton, stiffly. "I don't see that you need warn me."

"I thought we might as well have an understandin' about it," said the squire. "So you won't hire out the boy?"

"No, I cannot, under the circumstances. If I did I should consider his services worth more than two dollars a month."

"I might give him two'n a half," said the squire, fancying it was merely a question of money.

"How much do you pay Abner Kimball?"

"Wal, rather more than that," answered the squire, slowly.

"You pay him ten dollars a month, don't you?"

"Wal, somewheres about that; but it's more'n he earns."

"If he is worth ten dollars, Harry would be worth four or six."

"I'll give three," said the squire, who reflected that even at that rate he would be saving considerable.

"I will leave it to Harry himself," said his father.

"Harry, you hear Squire Green's offer. What do you say? Will you go to work for him at three dollars a month?"

"I'd rather go away, as you told me I might, father."

"You hear the boy's decision, squire."

"Wal, wal," said the squire, a good deal disappointed--for, to tell the truth, he had told Abner he should not want him, having felt confident of obtaining Harry. "I hope you won't neither of ye regret it."

His tone clearly indicated that he really hoped and expected they would. "I bid ye good night."

"I'll hev the cow back ag'in," said the squire to himself. "He needn't hope no massy. If he don't hev the money ready for me when the time is up, he shan't keep her."

The next morning he was under the unpleasant necessity of reengaging Abner.

"Come to think on't, Abner," he said, "I guess I'd like to hev you stay longer.

There's more work than I reckoned, and I guess I'll hev to have somebody."

This was at the breakfast table. Abner looked around him, and after making sure that there was nothing eatable left, put down his knife and fork with the air of one who could have eaten more, and answered, deliberately: "Ef I stay I'll hev to hev more wages."

"More wages?" repeated Squire Green, in dismay. "More'n ten dollars?"

"Yes, a fellow of my age orter hey more'n that."

"Ten dollars is a good deal of money."

"I can't lay up a cent off'n it."

"Then you're extravagant."

"No I ain't. I ain't no chance to be. My cousin, Paul Bickford, is gettin' fifteen dollars, and he ain't no better worker'n I am."

"Fifteen dollars!" ejaculated, the squire, as if he were naming some extraordinary sum. "I never heerd of such a thing."

"I'll work for twelve'n a half," said Abner, "and I won't work for no less."

"It's too much," said the squire. "Besides, you agreed to come for ten."

"I know I did; but this is a new engagement."

Finally Abner reduced his terms to twelve dollars, an advance of two dollars a month, to which the squire was forced to agree, though very reluctantly. He thought, with an inward groan, that but for his hasty dismissal of Abner the night before, on the supposition that he could obtain Harry in his place, he would not have been compelled to raise Abner's wages. This again resulted indirectly from selling the cow, which had put the new plan into his head. When the squire reckoned up this item, amounting in six months to twelve dollars, he began to doubt whether his cow trade had been quite so good after all.

"I'll get it out of Hiram Walton some way," he muttered. "He's a great fool to let that boy have his own way. I thought to be sure he'd oblige me arter the favor I done him in sellin' him the cow. There's gratitude for you!"

The squire's ideas about gratitude, and the manner in which he had earned it, were slightly mixed, it must be acknowledged. But, though he knew very well that he had been influenced only by the consideration of his own interest, he had a vague idea that he was entitled to some credit for his kindness in consenting to sell his neighbor a cow at an extortionate price.

Harry breathed a deep sigh of relief after Squire Green left the room.

"I was afraid you were going to hire me out to the squire, father," he said.

"You didn't enjoy the prospect, did you?" said his father, smiling.

"Not much."

"Shouldn't think he would," said his brother Tom.

"The squire's awful stingy. Abner Kimball told me he had the meanest break-fast he ever ate anywhere."

"I don't think any of his household are in danger of contracting the gout from luxurious living."

"I guess not," said Tom.

"I think," said Jane, slyly, "you'd better hire out Tom to the squire."

"The squire would have the worst of the bargain," said his father, with a good-natured hit at Tom's sluggishness.

"He wouldn't earn his board, however poor it might be."

"The squire didn't seem to like it very well," said Mrs. Walton, looking up from her mending.

"No, he fully expected to get Harry for little or nothing. It was ridiculous to offer two dollars a month for a boy of his age."

"I am afraid he will be more disposed to be hard on you, when the time comes to pay for the cow. He told you he wouldn't extend the time."

"He is not likely to after this; but, wife, we won't borrow trouble. Something may turn up to help us."

"I am sure I shall be able to help you about it, father," said Harry.

"I hope so, my son, but don't feel too certain. You may not succeed as well as you anticipate."

"I know that, but I mean to try at any rate."

"If you don't, Tom will," said his sister.

"Quit teasin' a feller, Jane," said Tom. "I ain't any lazier'n you are. If I am, I'll eat my head."

"Then you'll have to eat it, Tom," retorted Jane; "and it won't be much loss to you, either."

"Don't dispute, children," said Mrs. Walton. "I expect you both will turn over a new leaf by and by."

Meanwhile, Harry was busily reading the "Life of Franklin." The more he read, the more hopeful he became as to the future.

CHAPTER IX
LEAVING HOME

Monday morning came, and the whole family stood on the grass plat in front of the house, ready to bid Harry good-by. He was encumbered by no trunk, but carried his scanty supply of clothing wrapped in a red cotton handkerchief, and not a very heavy bundle at that. He had cut a stout stick in the woods near by, and from the end of this suspended over his back bore the bundle which contained all his worldly fortune except the twenty-five cents which was in his vest pocket.

"I don't like to have you go," said his mother, anxiously. "Suppose you don't get work?"

"Don't worry about me, mother," said Harry, brightly. "I'll get along some-how."

"Remember you've got a home here, Harry, whatever happens," said his father.

"I shan't forget, father."

"I wish I was going with you," said Tom, for the first time fired with the spirit of adventure.

"What could you do, Tom?" said Jane, teasingly.

"Work, of course."

"I never saw you do it yet."

"I'm no more lazy than you," retorted Tom, offended.

"Don't dispute, children, just as your brother is leaving us," said Mrs. Walton.

"Good-by, mother," said Harry, feeling an unwonted moistening of the eyes, as he reflected that he was about to leave the house in which he had lived since infancy.

"Good-by, my dear child," said his mother, kissing him.

"Be sure to write."

"Yes I will."

So with farewell greetings Harry walked out into the world. He had all at once assumed a man's responsibilities, and his face grew serious, as he began to realize that he must now look out for himself.

His native village was situated in the northern part of New Hampshire. Not far away could be seen, indistinct in the distance, the towering summits of the White Mountain range, but his back was turned to them. In the south were larger and more thriving villages, and the wealth was greater. Harry felt that his chances would be greater there. Not that he had any particular place in view. Wherever there was an opening, he meant to stop.

"I won't come back till I am better off," he said to himself. "If I don't succeed it won't be for want of trying."

He walked five miles without stopping. This brought him to the middle of the next town. He was yet on familiar ground, for he had been here more than once. He felt tired, and sat down by the roadside to rest before going farther. While he sat there the doctor from his own village rode by, and chanced to espy Harry, whom he recognized.

"What brings you here, Harry?" he asked, stopping his chaise.

"I'm going to seek my fortune," said Harry.

"What, away from home?"

"Yes, sir."

"I hadn't heard of that," said the doctor, surprised.

"You haven't run away from home?" he asked, with momentary suspicion.

"No, indeed!" said Harry, half indignantly. "Father's given his permission for me to go."

"Where do you expect to go?"

"South," said Harry, vaguely.

"And what do you expect to find to do?"

"I don't know--anything that'll bring me a living."

"I like your spunk," said the doctor, after a pause. "If you're going my way, as I suppose you are, I can carry you a couple of miles. That's better than walking, isn't it?"

"I guess it is," said Harry, jumping to his feet with alacrity.

In a minute he was sitting beside Dr. Dunham in his old-fashioned chaise. "I might have known that you were not running away," said the doctor. "I should be more likely to suspect your Brother Tom."

"Tom's too lazy to run away to earn his own living," said Harry, laughing, "as long as he can get it at home."

The doctor smiled.

"And what put it into your head to start out in this way?" he asked.

"The first thing, was reading the' Life of Franklin.'"

"To be sure. I remember his story."

"And the next thing was, because my father is so poor. He finds it hard work to support us all. The farm is small, and the land is poor. I want to help him if I can."

"Very commendable, Harry," said the doctor, kindly.

"You owe a debt of gratitude to your good father, who has not succeeded so well in life as he deserves."

"That's true, sir. He has always been a hard-working man."

"If you start out with such a good object, I think you will succeed. Have you any plans at all, or any idea what you would like to do?"

"I thought I should like to work in a shoe shop, if I got a chance," said Harry.

"You like that better than working on a farm, then?"

"Yes, sir, There isn't much money to be earned by working on a farm. I had a chance to do that before I came away."

"You mean working on your father's land, I suppose?"

"No, Squire Green wanted to hire me."

"What wages did he offer?"

"Two dollars a month, at first. Afterwards he got up to three."

The doctor smiled.

"How could you decline such a magnificent offer?" he asked.

"I don't think I should like boarding at the squire's."

"A dollar is twice as large at least in his eyes as in those of anyone else."

By this time they had reached a place where a road turned at right angles.

"I am going down here, Harry," said the doctor. "I should like to have you ride farther, but I suppose it would only be taking you out of your course."

"Yes, doctor. I'd better get out."

"I'll tell your father I saw you."

"Tell him I was in good spirits," said Harry, earnestly. "Mother'll be glad to know that."

"I will certainly. Good-by!"

"Good-by, doctor. Thank you for the ride."

"You are quite welcome to that, Harry."

Harry followed with his eyes the doctor's chaise. It seemed like severing the last link that bound him to his native village. He was very glad to have fallen in with the doctor, but it seemed all the more lonesome that he had left him.

Harry walked six miles farther, and then decided that it was time to rest again. He was not only somewhat fatigued, but decidedly hungry, although it was but eleven o'clock in the forenoon. However, it must be considered that he had walked eleven miles, and this was enough to give anyone an appetite.

He sat down again beside the road, and untying the handkerchief which contained his worldly possessions, he drew therefrom a large slice of bread and began to eat with evident relish. There was a slice of cold meat also, which he found tasted particularly good.

"I wonder whether they are thinking of me at home," he said to himself.

They were thinking about him, and when an hour later the family gathered around the table, no one seemed to have much appetite. All looked sober, for all were thinking of the absent son and brother.

"I wish Harry was here," said Jane, at length, giving voice to the general feeling.

"Poor boy," sighed his mother. "I'm afraid he'll have a hard time. I wish he had stayed at home, or even have gone to Squire Green's to work. Then we could have seen him every day."

"I should have pitied him more if he had gone there than I do now," said his father. "Depend upon it, it; will be better for him in the end."

"I hope so," said his mother, dubiously.

"But you don't feel sure? Well, time will show. We shall hear from him before long."

We go back to Harry.

He rested for a couple of hours, sheltered from the sun by the foliage of the oak beneath which he had stretched himself. He whiled away the time by reading for the second time some parts of the "Life of Franklin," which he had brought away in his bundle, with his few other possessions. It seemed even more interesting to him now that he, too, like Franklin, had started out in quest for fortune.

He resumed walking, but we will not dwell upon the details of his journey. At six o'clock he was twenty-five miles from home. He had not walked much in the afternoon when, all at once, he was alarmed by the darkening of the sky. It was evident that a storm was approaching. He looked about him for shelter from the shower, and a place where he could pass the night.

CHAPTER X
THE GENERAL

The clouds were darkening, and the shower was evidently not far off. It was a solitary place, and no houses were to be seen near by. But nearly a quarter of a mile back Harry caught sight of a small house, and jumping over the fence directed his steps toward it. Five minutes brought him to it. It was small, painted red, originally, but the color had mostly been washed away. It was not upon a public road, but there was a narrow lane leading to it from the highway. Probably it was occupied by a poor family, Harry thought. Still it would shelter him from the storm which had even now commenced.

He knocked at the door.

Immediately it was opened and a face peered out--the face of a man advanced in years. It was thin, wrinkled, and haggard. The thin white hair, uncombed, gave a wild appearance to the owner, who, in a thin, shrill voice, demanded, "Who are you?"

"My name is Harry Walton."

"What do you want?"

"Shelter from the storm. It is going to rain."

"Come in," said the old man, and opening the door wider, he admitted our hero.

Harry found himself in a room very bare of furniture, but there was a log fire in the fireplace, and this looked comfortable and pleasant. He laid down his bundle, and drawing up a chair sat down by it, his host meanwhile watching him closely.

"Does he live alone, I wonder?" thought Harry.

He saw no other person about, and no traces of a woman's presence. The floor looked as if it had not been swept for a month, and probably it had not.

The old man sat down opposite Harry, and stared at him, till our hero felt somewhat embarrassed and uncomfortable.

"Why don't he say something?" thought Harry.

"He is a very queer old man."

After a while his host spoke.

"Do you know who I am?" he asked.

"No," said Harry, looking at him.

"You've heard of me often," pursued the old man.

"I didn't know it," answered Harry, beginning to feel curious.

"In history," added the other.

"In history?"

"Yes."

Harry began to look at him in increased surprise.

"Will you tell me your name, if it is not too much trouble," he asked, politely.

"I gained the victory of New Orleans," said the old man.

"I thought General Jackson did that," said Harry.

"You're right," said the old man, complacently. "I am General Jackson."

"But General Jackson is dead."

"That's a mistake," said the old man, quietly. "That's what they say in all the books, but it isn't true."

This was amusing, but it was also startling. Harry knew now that the old man was crazy, or at least a monomaniac, and, though he seemed harmless enough, it was of course possible that he might be dangerous. He was almost sorry that he had sought shelter here. Better have encountered the storm in its full fury than place himself in the power of a maniac. The rain was now falling in thick drops, and he decided at any rate to remain a while longer. He knew that it would not be well to dispute the old man, and resolved to humor his delusion.

"You were President once, I believe?" he asked.

"Yes," said the old man; "and you won't tell anybody, will you?"

"No."

"I mean to be again," said the old man in a low voice, half in a whisper. "But you mustn't say anything about it. They'd try to kill me, if they knew it."

"Who would?"

"Mr. Henry Clay, and the rest of them."

"Doesn't Henry Clay want you to be President again?"

"Of course not. He wants to be President himself. That's why I'm hiding. They don't any of them know where I am. You won't tell, will you?"

"No."

"You might meet Henry Clay, you know."

Harry smiled to himself. It didn't seem very likely that he would ever find himself in such distinguished company, for Henry Clay was at that time living, and a United States Senator.

"What made you come here, General Jackson?" he inquired.

The old man brightened, on being called by this name.

"Because it was quiet. They can't find me here."

"When do you expect to be President again?"

"Next year," said the old man. "I've got it all arranged. My friends are to blow up the capitol, and I shall ride into Washington on a white horse. Do you want an office?"

"I don't know but I should like one," said Harry, amused.

"I'll see what I can do for you," said the old man, seriously. "I can't put you in my Cabinet. That's all arranged. If you would like to be Minister to England or to France, you can go."

"I should like to go to France. Benjamin Franklin was Minister to France."

"Do you know him?"

"No; but I have read his life."

"I'll put your name down in my book. What is it?"

"Harry Walton."

The old man went to the table, on which was a common account book. He took a pen, and, with a serious look, made this entry:

"I promise to make Harry Walton Minister to France, as soon as I take my place in the White House.

"GENERAL ANDREW JACKSON"

"It's all right now," he said.

"Thank you, general. You are very kind," said our hero.

"Were you ever a soldier?" asked his host.

"I never was."

"I thought you might have been in the battle of New Orleans. Our men fought splendidly, sir."

"I have no doubt of it."

"You'll read all about it in history. We fought behind cotton bales. It was glorious!"

"General," said Harry, "if you'll excuse me, I'll take out my supper from this bundle."

"No, no," said the old man; "you must take supper with me."

"I wonder whether he has anything fit to eat," thought Harry. "Thank you," he said aloud. "If you wish it."

The old man had arisen, and, taking a teakettle, suspended it over the fire. A monomaniac though he was on the subject of his identity with General Jackson, he knew how to make tea. Presently he took from the cupboard a baker's roll and some cold meat, and when the tea was ready, invited Harry to be seated at the table. Our hero did so willingly. He had lost his apprehensions, perceiving that his companion's lunacy was of a very harmless character.

"What if mother could see me now!" he thought.

Still the rain poured down. It showed no signs of slackening. He saw that it would be necessary to remain where he was through the night.

"General, can you accommodate me till morning?" he asked.

"Certainly," said the old man. "I shall be glad to have you stay here. Do you go to France to-morrow?"

"I have not received my appointment yet."

"True, true; but it won't be long. I will write your instructions to-night."

"Very well."

The supper was plain enough, but it was relished by our young traveler, whose long walk had stimulated a naturally good appetite.

"Eat heartily, my son," said the old man. "A long journey is before you."

After the meal was over, the old man began to write.

Harry surmised that it was his instructions. He paid little heed, but fixed his eyes upon the fire, listening to the rain that continued to beat against the window panes, and began to speculate about the future. Was he to be successful or not? He was not without solicitude, but he felt no small measure of hope. At nine o'clock he began to feel drowsy, and intimated as much to his host. The old man conducted him to an upper chamber, where there was a bed upon the floor.

"You can sleep there," he said.

"Where do you sleep?" asked Harry.

"Down below; but I shall not go to bed till late. I must get ready your instructions."

"Very well," said Harry. "Good night."

"Good night."

"I am glad he is not in the room with me," thought Harry. "I don't think there is any danger, but it isn't comfortable to be too near a crazy man."

CHAPTER XI
IN SEARCH OF WORK

When Harry awoke the next morning, after a sound and refreshing sleep, the sun was shining brightly in at the window. He rubbed his eyes, and stared about him, not at first remembering where he was. But almost immediately recollection came to his aid, and he smiled as he thought of the eccentric old man whose guest he was. He leaped out of bed, and quickly dressing himself, went downstairs. The fire was burning, and breakfast was already on the table. It was precisely similar to the supper of the night previous. The old man sat at the fireside smoking a pipe.

"Good morning, general," said Harry. "I am up late."

"It is no matter. You have a long journey before you, and it is well to rest before starting."

"Where does he think I am going?" thought our hero.

"Breakfast is ready," said the old man, hospitably. "I can't entertain you now as I could have done when I was President. You must come and see me at the White House next year."

"I should like to."

Harry ate a hearty breakfast. When it was over, he rose to go.

"I must be going, general," he said. "Thank you for your kind entertainment. If you would allow me to pay you."

"General Jackson does not keep an inn," said the old man, with dignity. "You are his guest. I have your instructions ready."

He opened a drawer in the table, and took a roll of foolscap, tied with a string.

"Put it in your bundle," he said. "Let no one see it. Above all, don't let it fall into the hands of Henry Clay, or my life will be in peril."

Harry solemnly assured him that Henry Clay should never see it, and shaking the old man by the hand, made his way across the fields to the main road. Looking back from time to time, he saw the old man watching him from his place in the doorway, his eyes shaded by his hand.

"He is the strangest man I ever saw," thought Harry. "Still he treated me kindly. I should like to find out some more about him."

When he reached the road he saw, just in front of him, a boy of about his own age driving half a dozen cows before him.

"Perhaps he can tell me something about the old man."

"Hello!" he cried, by way of salutation.

"Hello!" returned the country boy. "Where are you going?"

"I don't know. Wherever I can find work," answered our hero.

The boy laughed. "Dad finds enough for me to do. I don't have to go after it. Haven't you got a father?"

"Yes."

"Why don't you work for him?"

"I want to work for pay."

"On a farm?"

"No. I'll work in a shoe shop if I get a chance or in a printing office."

"Do you understand the shoe business?"

"No; but I can learn."

"Where did you come from?"

"Granton."

"You didn't come from there this morning?"

"No, I guess not, as it's over twenty miles. Last night I stopped at General Jackson's."

The boy whistled.

"What, at the old crazy man's that lives down here a piece?"

"Yes."

"What made you go there?"

"It began, to rain, and I had no other place to go."

"What did he say?" asked the new boy with curiosity.

"Did he cut up?"

"Cut up? No, unless you mean the bread. He cut up that."

"I mean, how did he act?"

"All right, except when he was talking about being General Jackson."

"Did you sleep there?"

"Yes."

"I wouldn't."

"Why not?"

"I wouldn't sleep in a crazy man's house."

"He wouldn't hurt you."

"I don't know about that. He chases us boys often, and threatens to kill us."

"You plague him, don't you?"

"I guess we do. We call him 'Old Crazy,' and that makes him mad. He says Henry Clay puts us up to it--ho, ho, ho!"

"He thinks Clay is his enemy. He told me so."

"What did you say?"

"Oh, I didn't contradict him. I called him general. He treated me tip-top. He is going to make me Minister of France, when he is President again."

"Maybe that was the best way to get along."

"How long has he lived here? What made him crazy?"

"I don't know. Folks say he was disappointed."

"Did he ever see Jackson?"

"Yes; he fit at New Orleans under him."

"Has he lived long around here?"

"Ever since I can remember. He gets a pension, I've heard father say. That's what keeps him."

Here the boy reached the pasture to which he was driving the cows, and Harry, bidding him "good-by," went on his way. He felt fresh and vigorous, and walked ten miles before he felt the need of rest. When this distance was accomplished, he found himself in the center of a good-sized village. He felt hungry, and the provision which he brought from home was nearly gone. There was a grocery store close at hand, and he went in, thinking that he would find something to help his meal. On the counter he saw some rolls, and there was an open barrel of apples not far off.

"What do you charge for your rolls?" he asked.

"Two cents."

"I'll take one. How do you sell your apples?"

"A cent apiece."

"I'll take two."

Thus for four cents Harry made quite a substantial addition to his meal. As he left the store, and walked up the road, with the roll in his hand, eating an apple, he called to mind Benjamin Franklin's entrance of Philadelphia with a roll under each arm.

"I hope I shall have as good luck as Franklin had," he thought.

Walking slowly, he saw, on a small building which he I had just reached, the sign, "Post Office."

"Perhaps the postmaster will know if anybody about here wants a boy," Harry said to himself. "At any rate, it won't do any harm to inquire."

He entered, finding himself in a small room, with one part partitioned off as a repository for mail matter. He stepped up to a little window, and presently the postmaster, an elderly man, presented himself.

"What name," he asked.

"I haven't come for a letter," said Harry.

"What do you want, then?" asked the official, but not roughly.

"Do you know of anyone that wants to hire a boy?"

"Who's the boy?"

"I am. I want to get a chance to work."

"What kind of work?"

"Any kind that'll pay my board and a little over."

"I don't know of any place," said the postmaster, after a little thought.

"Isn't there any shoe shop where I could get in?"

"That reminds me--James Leavitt told me this morning that his boy was going to Boston to go into a store in a couple of months. He's been pegging for his father and I guess they'll have to get somebody in his place."

Harry's face brightened at this intelligence.

"That's just the kind of place I'd like to get," he said.

"Where does Mr. Leavitt live?"

"A quarter of a mile from here--over the bridge. You'll know it well enough. It's a cottage house, with a shoe shop in the backyard."

"Thank you, sir," said Harry. "I'll go there and try my luck."

"Wait a minute," said the postmaster. "There's a letter here for Mr. Leavitt. If you're going there, you may as well carry it along. It's from Boston. I shouldn't wonder if it's about the place Bob Leavitt wants."

"I'll take it with pleasure," said Harry.

It occurred to him that it would be a good introduction for him, and pave the way for his application.

"I hope I may get a chance to work for this Mr. Leavitt," he said to himself. "I like the looks of this village. I should like to live here for a while."

He walked up the street, crossing the bridge referred to by the postmaster, and looked carefully on each side of him for the cottage and shop. At length he came to a place which answered the description, and entered the yard. As he neared the shop he heard a noise which indicated that work was going on inside. He opened the door, and entered.

CHAPTER XII
THE NEW BOARDER

Harry found himself in a room about twenty-five feet by twenty. The floor was covered with scraps of leather. Here stood a deep wooden box containing a case of shoes ready to send off. There was a stove in the center, in which, however, as it was a warm day, no fire was burning. There were three persons present. One, a man of middle age, was Mr. James Leavitt, the proprietor of the shop. His son Robert, about seventeen, worked at an adjoining bench. Tom Gavitt, a journeyman, a short, thick-set man of thirty, employed by Mr. Leavitt, was the third.

The three looked up as Harry entered the shop.

"I have a letter for Mr. Leavitt," said our hero.

"That is my name," said the eldest of the party.

Harry advanced, and placed it in his hands.

"Where did you get this letter?"

"At the post office."

"I can't call you by name. Do you live about here?"

"No, I came from Granton."

No further questions were asked just then, as Mr. Leavitt, suspending work, opened the letter.

"It's from your Uncle Benjamin," he said, addressing Robert. "Let us see what he has to say."

He read the letter in silence.

"What does he say, father?" asked Robert.

"He says he shall be ready to take you the first of September. That's in six weeks--a little sooner than we calculated. I wish it were a little later, as work is brisk, and I may find it difficult to fill your place without paying more than I want to."

"I guess you can pick up somebody," said Robert, who was anxious to go to Boston as soon as possible.

"Won't you hire me?" asked Harry, who felt that the time had come for him to announce his business.

Mr. Leavitt looked at him more attentively.

"Have you ever worked in a shop?"

"No, sir."

"It will take you some time to learn pegging."

"I'll work for my board till I've learned."

"But you won't be able to do all I want at first."

"Suppose I begin now," said Harry, "and work for my board till your son goes away. By that time I can do considerable."

"I don't know but that's a good idea," said Mr. Leavitt. "What do you think, Bob?"

"Better take him, father," said Robert, who felt that it would facilitate his own plans.

"How much would you want after you have learned?" asked the father.

"I don't know; what would be a fair price," said Harry.

"I'll give you three dollars a week and board," said Mr. Leavitt, after a little consideration--"that is, if I am satisfied with you."

"I'll come," said Harry, promptly. He rapidly calculated that there would be about twenty weeks for which he would receive pay before the six months expired, at the end of which the cow must be paid for. This would give him sixty dollars, of which he thought he should be able to save forty to send or carry to his father.

"How did you happen to come to me?" asked Mr. Leavitt, with some curiosity.

"I heard at the post office that your son was going to the city to work, and I thought I could get in here."

"Is your father living?"

"Yes, my father and mother both."

"What business is he in?"

"He is a farmer; but his farm is small, and not very profitable."

"So you thought you would leave home and try something else?"

"Yes, sir."

"Well, we will try you at shoemaking. Robert, you can teach him what you know about pegging."

"Come here," said Robert. "What is your name?"

"Harry Walton."

"How old are you?"

"Fifteen."

"Did you ever work much?"

"Yes, on a farm."

"Do you think you'll like shoemaking better?"

"I don't know yet, but I think I shall. I like almost anything better than farming."

"And I like almost anything better than pegging. I began when I was only twelve years old, and I'm sick of it."

"What kind of store is it you are going into?"

"Dry goods. My uncle, Benjamin Streeter, mother's brother, keeps a dry goods store on Washington street. It'll be jolly living in the city."

"I don't know," said Harry thoughtfully. "I think I like a village just as well."

"What sort of a place is Granton, where you come from?"

"It's a farming town. There isn't any village at all."

"There isn't much going on here."

"There'll be more than in Granton. There's nothing to do there but to work on a farm."

"I shouldn't like that myself; but the city's the best of all"

"Can you make more money in a store than working in a shoe shop?"

"Not so much at first, but after you've got learned there's better chances. There's a clerk, that went from here ten years ago, that gets fifty dollars a week."

"Does he?" asked Harry, to whose rustic inexperience this seemed like an immense salary. "I didn't think any clerk ever got so much."

"They get it often if they are smart," said Robert.

Here he was wrong, however. Such cases are exceptional, and a city fry goods clerk, considering his higher rate of expense, is no better off than many country mechanics. But country boys are apt to form wrong ideas on this subject, and are in too great haste to forsake good country homes for long hours of toil behind a city counter, and a poor home in a dingy, third-class city boarding house. It is only in the wholesale houses, for the most part, that high salaries are paid, and then, of course, only to those who have shown superior energy and capacity. Of course some do achieve success and become rich; but of the tens of thousand who come from the country to seek clerkships, but a very small proportion rise above a small income.

"I shall have a start," Robert proceeded, "for I go into my uncle's store. I am to board at his house, and get three dollars a week."

"That's what your father offers me," said Harry.

"Yes; you'll earn more after a while, and I can now; but I'd rather live in the city. There's lots to see in the city--theaters, circuses, and all kinds of amusements."

"You won't have much money to spend on theaters," said Harry, prudently.

"Not at first, but I'll get raised soon."

"I think I should try to save as much as I could."

"Out of three dollars a week?"

"Yes."

"What can you save out of that?"

"I expect to save half of it, perhaps more."

"I couldn't do that. I want a little fun."

"You see my father's poor. I want to help him all I can."

"That's good advice for you, Bob," said Mr. Leavitt.

"Save up money, and help me."

Robert laughed.

"You'll have to wait till I get bigger pay," he said.

"Your father's better off than mine," said Harry.

"Of course, if he don't need it, that makes a difference."

Here the sound of a bell was heard, proceeding from the house.

"Robert," said his father "go in and tell your mother to put an extra seat at the table. She doesn't know that we've got a new boarder."

He took off his apron, and washed his hands. Tom Gavitt followed his example, but didn't go into the house of his employer. He lived in a house of his own about five minutes' walk distant, but left the shop at the same time. In a country village the general dinner hour is twelve o'clock--a very unfashionably early hour--but I presume any of my readers who had been at work from seven o'clock would have no difficulty in getting up a good appetite at noon.

Robert went in and informed his mother of the new boarder. It made no difference, for the table was always well supplied.

"This is Harry Walton, mother," said Mr. Leavitt, "our new apprentice. He will take Bob's place when he goes."

"I am glad to see you," said Mrs. Leavitt, hospitably.

"You may sit here, next to Robert."

"What have you got for us to-day, mother?" asked her husband.

"A picked-up dinner. There's some cold beef left over from yesterday, and I've made an apple pudding."

"That's good. We don't want anything better."

So Harry thought. Accustomed to the painful frugality of the table at home, he regarded this as a splendid dinner, and did full justice to it.

In the afternoon he resumed work in the shop under Robert's guidance. He was in excellent spirits. He felt that he was very fortunate to have gained a place so soon, and determined to write home that same evening.

CHAPTER XIII
AN INVITATION DECLINED

The summer passed quickly, and the time arrived for Robert Leavitt to go to the city. By this time Harry was well qualified to take his place. It had not been difficult, for he had only been required to peg, and that is learned in a short time. Harry, however, proved to be a quick workman, quicker, if anything, than Robert, though the latter had been accustomed to the work for several years. Mr. Leavitt was well satisfied with his new apprentice, and quite content to pay him the three dollars a week agreed upon. In fact, it diminished the amount of cash he was called upon to pay.

"Good-by, Harry," said Robert, as he saw the coach coming up the road, to take him to the railroad station.

"Good-by, and good luck!" said Harry.

"When you come to the city, come and see me."

"I don't think I shall be going very soon. I can't afford it."

"You must save up your wages, and you'll have enough soon."

"I've got another use for my wages, Bob."

"To buy cigars?"

Harry shook his head. "I shall save it up to carry home."

"Well, you must try to make my place good in the shop."

"He can do that," said Mr. Leavitt, slyly; "but there's one place where he can't equal you."

"Where is that?"

"At the dinner table."

"You've got me there, father," said Bob, good-naturedly. "Well, good-by all, here's the stage."

In a minute more he was gone. Harry felt rather lonely, for he had grown used to working beside him. But his spirits rose as he reflected that the time had now come when he should be in receipt of an income. Three dollars a week made him feel rich in anticipation. He looked forward already with satisfaction to the time when he might go home with money enough to pay off his father's debt to Squire Green. But he was not permitted to carry out his economical purpose without a struggle.

On Saturday evening, after he had received his week's pay, Luke Harrison, who worked in a shop near by, met him at the post office.

"Come along, Harry," he said. "Let us play a game of billiards."

"You must excuse me," said Harry.

"Oh, come along," said Luke, taking him by the arm; "it's only twenty-five cents."

"I can't afford it,"

"Can't afford it! Now that's nonsense. You just changed a two-dollar note for those postage stamps."

"I know that; but I must save that money for another purpose."

"What's the use of being stingy, Harry? Try one game."

"You can get somebody else to play with you, Luke."

"Oh, hang it, if you care so much for a quarter, I'll pay for the game myself. Only come and play."

Harry shook his head.

"I don't want to amuse myself at your expense."

"You are a miser," said Luke, angrily.

"You can call me so, if you like," said Harry, firmly; "but that won't make it so."

"I don't see how you can call yourself anything else, if you are so afraid to spend your money."

"I have good reasons."

"What are they?"

"I told you once that I had another use for the money."

"To hoard away in an old stocking," said Luke, sneering.

"You may say so, if you like," said Harry, turning away.

He knew he was right, but it was disagreeable to be called a miser. He was too proud to justify himself to Luke, who spent all his money foolishly, though earning considerably larger wages than he.

There was one thing that Harry had not yet been able to do to any great extent, though it was something he had at heart. He had not forgotten his motto, "Live and Learn," and now that he was in a fair way to make a living, he felt that he had made no advance in learning during the few weeks since he arrived in Glenville.

The day previous he had heard, for the first time, that there was a public library in another part of the town, which was open evenings. Though it was two miles distant, and he had been at work all day, he determined to walk up there and get a book. He felt that he was very ignorant, and that his advance in the world depended upon his improving all opportunities that might present themselves for extending his limited knowledge. This was evidently one.

After his unsatisfactory interview with Luke, he set out for the upper village, as it was called. Forty minutes' walk brought him to the building in which the library was kept. An elderly man had charge of it--a Mr. Parmenter.

"Can I take out a book?" asked Harry.

"Do you live in town?"

"Yes, sir."

"I don't remember seeing you before. You don't live in this village, do you?"

"No, sir. I live in the lower village."

"What is your name?"

"Harry Walton."

"I don't remember any Walton family."

"My father lives in Granton. I am working for Mr. James Leavitt."

"I have no doubt this is quite correct, but I shall have to have Mr. Leavitt's certificate to that effect, before I can put your name down, and trust you with books."

"Then can't I take any book to-night?" asked Harry, disappointed.

"I am afraid not."

So it seemed his two-mile walk was for nothing. He must retrace his steps and come again Monday night.

He was turning away disappointed when Dr. Townley, of the lower village, who lived near Mr. Leavitt, entered the library.

"My wife wants a book in exchange for this, Mr. Parmenter," he said. "Have you got anything new in? Ah, Harry Walton, how came you here? Do you take books out of the library?"

"That's is what I came up for, but the librarian says I must bring a line from Mr. Leavitt, telling who I am."

"If Dr. Townley knows you, that is sufficient," said the librarian.

"He is all right, Mr. Parmenter. He is a young neighbor of mine."

"That is enough. He can select a book."

Harry was quite relieved at this fortunate meeting, and after a little reflection selected the first volume of "Rollin's Universal History," a book better known to our fathers than the present generation.

"That's a good, solid book, Harry," said the doctor.

"Most of our young people select stories."

"I like stories very much," said Harry; "but I have only a little time to read, and I must try to learn something."

"You are a sensible boy," said the doctor, emphatically.

"I'm afraid there are few of our young people who take such wise views of what is best for them. Most care only for present enjoyment."

"I have got my own way to make," said Harry, "and I suppose that is what influences me. My father is poor and cannot help me, and I want to rise in the world."

"You are going the right way to work. Do you intend to take out books often from the library?"

"Yes, sir."

"It will be a long walk from the lower village."

"I would walk farther rather than do without the books."

"I can save you at any rate from walking back. My chaise is outside, and, if you will jump in, I will carry you home."

"Thank you, doctor. I shall be very glad to ride."

On the way, Dr. Townley said: "I have a few miscellaneous book in my medical library, which I will lend to you with pleasure, if you will come in. It may save you an occasional walk to the library."

Harry thanked him, and not long afterwards availed himself of the considerate proposal. Dr Townley was liberally educated, and as far as his professional engagements would permit kept up with general literature. He gave Harry some valuable directions as to the books which it would benefit him to read, and more than once took him up on the road to the library.

Once a week regularly Harry wrote home. He knew that his letters would give pleasure to the family, and he never allowed anything to interfere with his duty.

His father wrote: "We are getting on about as usual. The cow does tolerably well, but is not as good as the one I lost. I have not yet succeeded in laying up anything toward paying for her. Somehow, whenever I have a few dollars laid aside Tom wants shoes, or your sister wants a dress, or some other expense swallows it up."

Harry wrote in reply: "Don't trouble yourself, father, about your debt to Squire Green. If I have steady work, and keep my health, I shall have enough to pay it by the time it comes due."

CHAPTER XIV
THE TAILOR'S CUSTOMER

At the end of six weeks from the date of Robert's departure, Harry had been paid eighteen dollars. Of this sum he had spent but one dollar, and kept the balance in his pocketbook. He did not care to send it home until he had enough to meet Squire Green's demand, knowing that his father would be able to meet his ordinary expenses. Chiefly through the reports of Luke Harrison he was acquiring the reputation of meanness, though, as we know, he was far from deserving it.

"See how the fellow dresses," said Luke, contemptuously, to two of his companions one evening. "His clothes are shabby enough, and he hasn't got an overcoat at all. He hoards his money, and is too stingy to buy one. See, there he comes, buttoned to the chin to keep warm, and I suppose he has more money in his pocketbook than the whole of us together. I wouldn't be as mean as he is for a hundred dollars."

"You'd rather get trusted for your clothes than do without them," said Frank Heath, slyly; for he happened to know that Luke had run up a bill with the tailor, about which the latter was getting anxious.

"What if I do," said Luke, sharply, "as long as I am going to pay for them?"

"Oh, nothing," said Frank. "I didn't say anything against it, did I? I suppose you are as able to owe the tailor as anyone."

By this time, Harry had come up.

"Where are you going, Walton?" asked Luke. "You look cold."

"Yes, it's a cold day."

"Left your overcoat at home, didn't you?"

Harry colored. The fact was, he felt the need of an overcoat, but didn't know how to manage getting one. At the lowest calculation, it would cost all the money he had saved up for one, and the purchase would defeat all his plans. The one he had worn at home during the previous winter was too small for him, and had been given to his brother.

"If I only could get through the winter without one," he thought, "I should be all right." But a New England winter is not to be braved with impunity, useless protected by adequate clothing. Luke's sneer was therefore not without effect. But he answered, quietly: "I did not leave it at home, for I have none to leave."

"I suppose you are bound to the tailor's to order one."

"What makes you think so?" asked Harry.

"You are not such a fool as to go without one when you have money in your pocket, are you?"

"You seem very curious about my private affairs," said Harry, rather provoked.

"He's only drumming up customers for the tailor," said Frank Heath. "He gets a commission on all he brings."

"That's the way he pays his bill," said Sam Anderson.

"Quit fooling, boys," said Luke, irritated. "I ain't a drummer. I pay my bills, like a gentleman."

"By keeping the tailor waiting," said Frank.

"Quit that!"

So attention was diverted from Harry by this opportune attack upon Luke, much to our hero's relief. Nevertheless, he saw, that in order to preserve his health, he must have some outer garment, and in order the better to decide what to do, he concluded to step into the tailor's, and inquire his prices.

The tailor, Merrill by name, had a shop over the dry goods store, and thither Harry directed his steps. There was one other person in the shop, a young fellow but little larger than Harry, though two years older, who was on a visit to an aunt in the neighborhood, but lived in Boston. He belonged to a rich family, and had command of considerable money. His name was Maurice Tudor. He had gone into the shop to leave a coat to be repaired.

"How are you, Walton?" he said, for he knew our hero slightly.

"Pretty well. Thank you."

"It's pretty cold for October."

"Yes, unusually so."

"Mr. Merrill," said Harry, "I should like to inquire the price of an overcoat. I may want to order one by and by."

"What sort of one do you want--pretty nice?"

"No, I can't afford anything nice--something as cheap as possible."

"This is the cheapest goods I have," said the tailor, pointing to some coarse cloth near by.

"I can make you up a coat from that for eighteen dollars."

"Eighteen dollars!" exclaimed Harry, in dismay. "Is that the cheapest you have?"

"The very cheapest."

After a minute's pause he added, "I might take off a dollar for cash. I've got enough of running up bills. There's Luke Harrison owes me over thirty dollars, and I don't believe he means to pay it al all."

"If I buy, I shall pay cash," said Harry, quietly.

"You can't get anything cheaper than this." said the tailor.

"Very likely not," said Harry, soberly. "I'll think about it, and let you know if I decide to take it."

Maurice Tudor was a silent listener to this dialogue. He saw Harry's sober expression, and he noticed the tone in which he repeated "eighteen dollars," and he guessed the truth. He lingered after Harry went out, and said:

"That's a good fellow."

"Harry Walton?" repeated the tailor. "Yes, he's worth a dozen Luke Harrisons."

"Has he been in the village long?"

"No, not more than two or three months. He works for Mr. Leavitt."

"He is rather poor, I suppose."

"Yes. The boys call him mean; but Leavitt tells me he is saving up every cent to send to his father, who is a poor farmer."

"That's a good thing in him."

"Yes, I wish I could afford to give him and overcoat. He needs one, but I suppose seventeen dollars will come rather hard on him to pay. If it was Luke Harrison, it wouldn't trouble him much."

"You mean he would get it on tick."

"Yes, if he found anybody fool enough to trust him. I've done it as long as I'm going to. He won't get a dollar more credit out of me till he pays his bill."

"You're perfectly right, there."

"So I think. He earns a good deal more than Walton, but spends what he earns on billiards, drinks and cigars."

"There he comes up the stairs, now."

In fact, Luke with his two companions directly afterwards entered the shop.

"Merrill," said he, "have you got in any new goods? I must have a new pair of pants."

"Yes, I've got some new goods. There's a piece open before you."

"It's a pretty thing, Merrill," said Luke, struck by it; "what's your price for a pair off of it?"

"Ten dollars."

"Isn't that rather steep?"

"No; the cloth is superior quality."

"Well, darn the expense. I like it, and must have it. Just measure me, will you?"

"Are you ready to pay the account I have against you?"

"How much is it?"

The tailor referred to his books.

"Thirty-two dollars and fifty cents," he answered.

"All right, Merrill. Wait till the pants are done, and I'll pay the whole at once."

"Ain't my credit good?" blustered Luke.

"You can make it good," said the tailor, significantly.

"I didn't think you'd make such a fuss about a small bill."

"I didn't think you'd find is so difficult to pay a small bill," returned the tailor.

Luke looked discomfited. He was silent a moment, and then changed his tactics.

"Come, Merrill," he said, persuasively; "don't be alarmed. I'm good for it, I guess. I haven't got the money convenient to-day. I lent fifty dollars. I shall have it back next week and then I will pay you."

"I am glad to hear it," said Merrill.

"So just measure me and hurry up the pants."

"I'm sorry but I can't till you settle the bill."

"Look here, has Walton been talking against me?"

"No; what makes you think so?"

"He don't like me, because I twitted him with his meanness."

"I don't consider him mean."

"Has he ever bought anything of you?"

"No."

"I knew it. He prefers to go ragged and save his money."

"He's too honorable to run up a bill without paying it."

"Do you mean me?" demanded Luke, angrily.

"I hope not. I presume you intend to pay your bills."

Luke Harrison left the shop. He saw that he exhausted his credit with Merrill. As to paying the bill, there was not much chance of that at present, as he had but one dollar and a half in his pocket.

CHAPTER XV
"BY EXPRESS"

There's a model for you," said the tailor to Maurice Tudor. "He won't pay his bills."

"How did you come to trust him in the first place?"

"I didn't know him then as well as I do now. I make it a practice to accommodate my customers by trusting them for a month or two, if they want it. But Luke Harrison isn't one to be trusted."

"I should say not."

"If young Walton wants to get an overcoat on credit, I shan't object. I judge something by looks, and I am sure he is honest."

"Well, good night, Mr. Merrill. You'll have my coat done soon?"

"Yes, Mr. Tudor. It shall be ready for you to-morrow."

Maurice Tudor left the tailor's shop, revolving a new idea which had just entered his mind. Now he remembered that he had at home and excellent overcoat which he had worn the previous winter, but which was now too small for him. He had no younger brother to wear it, nor in his circumstances was such economy necessary. As well as he could judge by observing Harry's figure, it would be an excellent fit for him. Why should he not give it to him?

The opportunity came. On his way home he overtook our hero, plunged in thought. In fact, he was still occupied with the problem of the needed overcoat.

"Good evening, Harry," said young Tudor.

"Good evening, Mr. Tudor," answered Harry. "Are you going back to the city soon?"

"In the course of a week or two. Mr. Leavitt's son is in a store in Boston, is he not?"

"Yes. I have taken his place in the shop."

"By the way, I saw you in Merrill's this evening."

"Yes; I was pricing an overcoat."

"I bought this one in Boston just before I came away. I have a very good one left from last winter but it is too small for me. It is of no use to me. If I thought you would accept it, I would offer it to you."

Harry's heart gave a joyful bound.

"Accept it!" he repeated. "Indeed I will and thank you for your great kindness."

"Then I will write home at once to have it sent to me. I also have a suit which I have outgrown; if you wouldn't be too proud to take it."

"I am not so foolish. It will be a great favor."

"I thought you would take it right," said Maurice, well pleased. "I will also send for the suit. I will get my mother to forward them by express."

"They will be as good as money to me," said Harry; "and that is not very plenty with me."

"Will you tell me something of your circumstances? Perhaps I may have it in my power to help you."

Harry, assured of his friendly interest, did not hesitate to give him a full account of his plans in life, and especially of his desire to relieve his father of the burden of poverty. His straightforward narrative made a very favorable impression upon Maurice, who could not help reflecting: "How far superior this boy is to Luke Harrison and his tribe!"

"Thank you for telling me all this," he said. "It was not from mere curiosity that I asked."

"I am sure of that," said Harry. "Thanks to your generosity, I shall present a much more respectable appearance, besides being made more comfortable."

Three days later a large bundle was brought by the village expressman to Mr. Leavitt's door.

"A bundle for you, Walton," said the expressman, seeing Harry in the yard.

"What is there to pay?" he asked.

"Nothing. It was prepaid in the city?"

Harry took it up to his room and opened it eagerly. First came the promised overcoat. It was of very handsome French cloth, with a velvet collar, and rich silk facings, far higher in cost than any Mr. Merrill would have made for him. It fitted as if it had been made for him. Next came, not one, but two complete suits embracing coat, vest and pants. One of pepper-and-salt cloth, the other a dark blue. These, also, so similar was he in figure to Maurice, fitted him equally well. The clothes which he brought with from form Granton were not only of coarse material but were far from stylish in cut, whereas these garments had been made by a fashionable Boston tailor and set off his figure to much greater advantage.

"I wonder what Luke Harrison will say?" said our hero to himself, smiling, as he thought of the surprise of Luke at witnessing his transformation.

"I've a great mind to keep these on to-night," he said.

"Perhaps I shall meet Luke. He won't have anything more to say about my going without an overcoat."

After supper Harry, arrayed in his best suit and wearing the overcoat, walked down tot he center of the village.

Luke was standing on the piazza of the tavern.

"Luke, see how Walton is dressed up!" exclaimed Frank Heath, who was the first to see our hero.

"Dressed up!" repeated Luke, who was rather shortsighted. "That would be a good joke."

"He's got a splendid overcoat," continued Frank.

"Where'd he get it? Merrill hasn't been making him one."

"It's none of Merrill's work. It's too stylish for him."

By this time Harry had come within Luke's range of vision. The latter surveyed him with astonishment and it must be confessed, with disappointment; for he had been fond of sneering at Harry's clothes, and now the latter was far better dressed than himself.

"Where did you get that coat, Walton?" asked Luke, the instant Harry came up.

"Honestly," said Harry, shortly.

"Have you got anything else new?"

Harry opened his coat and displayed the suit.

"Well, you are coming out, Walton, that's a fact," said Frank Heath. "That's a splendid suit."

"I thought you couldn't afford to buy a coat," said Luke.

"You see I've got one," answered Harry.

"How much did it cost?"

"That's a secret."

Here he left Luke and Frank.

"Well, Luke, what do you say to that?" said Frank Heath.

Luke said nothing. He was astonished and unhappy. He had a fondness for dress and spent a good share of his earnings upon it, paying where he must, and getting credit besides where he could. But he had never had so stylish a suit as this and it depressed him.

CHAPTER XVI
ASKING A FAVOR

There was one other tailor in the village, James Hayden, and to him Luke Harrison determined to transfer his custom, hoping to be allowed to run up a bill with him. He did not like his style of cut as well as Merrill's, but from the latter he was cut off unless he would pay the old bill, and this would be inconvenient.

He strolled into James Hayden's shop and asked to look at some cloth for pants.

Hayden was a shrewd man and, knowing that Luke was a customer of his neighbor, suspected the reason of his transfer. However, he showed the cloth, and, a selection having been made, measured him.

"When will you have them done?" asked Luke.

"In three days."

"I want them by that time sure."

"Of course you pay cash."

"Why," said Luke, hesitating, "I suppose you won't mind giving me a month's credit."

Mr. Hayden shook his head.

"I couldn't do it. My goods are already paid for and I have to pay for the work. I must have cash."

"Merrill always trusted me," pleaded Luke.

"Then why did you leave him?"

"Why," said Luke, a little taken aback, "he didn't cut the last clothes exactly to suit me."

"Didn't suit you? I thought you young people preferred his cut to mine. I am old-fashioned. Hadn't you better go back to Merrill?"

"I've got tired of him," said Luke. "I'll get a pair of pants of you, and see how I like them."

"I'll make them but I can't trust."

"All right. I'll bring the money," said Luke, who yet thought that he might get off by paying part down when he took the pants.

"The old fellow's deuced disobliging," said he o Frank Heath, when they got into the street.

"I don't know as I blame him," said Frank.

"I wish Merrill wasn't so stiff about it. He's terribly afraid of losing his bill."

"That's where he's right," said Frank, laughing. "I'd be the same if I were in his place."

"Do you always pay your bills right off?" said Luke.

"Yes, I do. I don't pretend to be a model boy. I'm afraid I keep bad company," he continued, "but I don't owe a cent to anybody except for board and that I pay up at the end of every week."

Luke dropped the subject, not finding it to his taste.

On Saturday night he went round to the tailor's.

"Have you got my pants done, Mr. Hayden?"

"Yes--here they are."

"Let me see," he said, "how much are they?"

"Nine dollars."

"I'll pay you three dollars to-night and the rest at the end of next week," he said.

"Very well; then you may have them at the end of next week."

"Why not now? They are done, ain't they?"

"Yes," said Mr. Hayden; "but not paid for."

"Didn't I tell you I'd pay three dollars now?"

"Our terms are cash down."

"You ain't afraid of me, are you?" blustered Luke.

"You understood when you ordered the pants that they were to be paid for when they were taken."

"I hate to see people so afraid of losing their money."

"Do you? Was that why you left Merrill?"

Luke colored. He suspected that the fact of his unpaid bill at the other tailor's was known to Mr. Hayden.

"I've a great mind to leave them on your hands."

"I prefer to keep them on my hands, rather than to let them go out of the shop without being paid for."

"Frank," said Luke, turning to his companion, "lend me five dollars, can't you?"

"I'm the wrong fellow to ask," said he; "I've got to pay my board and another bill to-night."

"Oh, let your bills wait."

"And lend you the money? Thank you, I ain't so green. When should I get the money again?"

"Next week."

"In a horn. No; I want to wear the pants to-morrow. I'm going out to ride."

"I don't see, unless you fork over the spondulies."

"I can't. I haven't got enough money."

"See Harry Walton."

"I don't believe he has got any. He bought a lot of clothes last week. They must have cost a pile."

"Can't help it. I saw him open his pocketbook last night and in it was a roll of bills."

Turning to the tailor, Luke said: "Just lay aside the pants and I'll come back for them pretty soon."

Mr. Hayden smiled to himself.

"There's nothing like fetching up these fellows with a round turn," he said. "'No money, no clothes'--that's my motto. Merrill told me all about that little bill that sent Luke Harrison over here. He don't run up any bill with me, if I know myself."

Luke went round to the village store. Harry Walton usually spent a part of every evening in instructive reading and study; but after a hard day's work he felt it necessary to pass an hour or so in the open air, so he came down to the center of center of the village.

"Hello, Walton!" said Luke, accosting him with unusual cordiality. "You are just the fellow I want to see."

"Am I?" inquired Harry in surprise, for there was no particular friendship or intimacy between them.

"Yes; I'm going to ask a little favor of you--a mere trifle. Lend me five or ten dollars for a week. Five will do it, you can't spare more."

Harry shook his head.

"I can't do that, Luke."

"Why not? Haven't you got as much?"

"Yes, I've got it."

"Then why won't you lend it to me?"

"I have little money and I can't run any risk."

"Do you think I won't pay you back?"

"Why do you need to borrow of me? You get much higher wages than I do."

"I want to pay a bill to-night. I didn't think you'd be so unaccommodating."

"I shouldn't be willing to lend to anyone," said Harry.

"The money isn't mine. I am going to send it home."

"A great sight you are!" sneered Luke. "I wanted to see just how mean you were. You've got the money in your pocket but you won't lend it."

This taunt did not particularly disturb Harry. There is a large class like Luke, who offended at being refused a loan, though quite aware that they are never likely to repay it. My young readers will be sure to meet specimens of this class, against whom the only protection is a very firm and decided "No."

CHAPTER XVII
THE NIGHT SCHOLARS

Immediately after Thanksgiving Day, the winter schools commenced. That in the center district was kept by a student of Dartmouth college, who had leave of absence from the college authorities for twelve weeks, in order by teaching to earn something to help defray his college expenses. Leonard Morgan, now a junior, was a tall, strongly made young man of twenty-two, whose stalwart frame had not been reduced by his diligent study. There were several shoe shops in the village, each employing from one to three boys, varying in age from fifteen to nineteen. Why could he not form a private class, to meet in the evening, to be instructed in advanced arithmetic, or, if desired, in Latin and Greek? He broached the idea to Stephen Bates, the prudential committeeman.

"I don't know," said Mr. Bates, "what our boys will think of it. I've got a boy that I'll send, but whether you'll get enough to make it pay I don't know."

"I suppose I can have the schoolhouse, Mr. Bates?"

"Yes, there won't be no objection. Won't it be too much for you after teachin' in the daytime?"

"It would take a good deal to break me down."

"Then you'd better draw up a notice and put it up in the store and tavern," suggested the committeeman.

In accordance with this advice, the young teacher posted up in the two places the following notice:

"EVENING SCHOOL

"I propose to start an evening school for those who are occupied during the day, and unable to attend the district school. Instruction will be given in such English branches as may be desired, and also in Latin and Greek, if any are desirous of pursuing a classical course. The school will commence next Monday evening at the schoolhouse, beginning at seven o'clock. Terms: Seventy cents a week, or five dollars for the term of ten weeks.

"LEONARD MORGAN."

"Are you going to join the class, Walton?" asked Frank Heath.

"Yes," said Harry, promptly.

"Where'll you get the money?" asked Luke Harrison, in a jeering tone.

"I shan't have to go far for it."

"I don't see how you can spend so much money."

"I am willing to spend money when I can get my money's worth," said our hero. "Are you going?"

"To school? No, I guess not. I've got through my schooling."

"You don't know enough to hurt you, do you, Luke?" inquired Frank Heath, slyly.

"Nor I don't want to. I know enough to get along."

"I don't and never expect to," said Harry.

"Do you mean to go to school when you're a gray-headed old veteran?" asked Frank, jocosely.

"I may not go to school then but I shan't give up learning then," said Harry, smiling. "One can learn without going to school. But while I'm young, I mean to go to school as much as I can."

"I guess you're right," said Frank; "I'd go myself, only I'm too lazy. It's hard on a feller to worry his brain with study after he's been at work all day. I don't believe I was cut out for a great scholar."

"I don't believe you were, Frank," said Joe Bates.

"You always used to stand pretty well down toward the foot of the class when you went to school."

"A feller can't be smart as well as handsome. As long as I'm good-looking, I won't complain because I wasn't born with the genius of a Bates."

"Thank you for the compliment, Frank, though I suppose it means that I am homely. I haven't got any genius or education to spare."

When Monday evening arrived ten pupils presented themselves, of whom six were boys, or young men, and four were girls. Leonard Morgan felt encouraged. A class of ten, though paying but five dollars each, would give him fifty dollars, which would be quite an acceptable addition to his scanty means.

"I am glad to see so many," he said. "I think our evening class will be a success. I will take your names and ascertain what studies you wish to pursue."

When he came to Harry; he asked, "What do you propose to study?"

"I should like to take up algebra and Latin, if you are willing," answered our hero.

"Have you studied either at all?"

"No, sir; I have not had an opportunity."

"How far have you been in arithmetic?"

"Through the square and cube root?"

"If you have been so far, you will have no difficulty with algebra. As to Latin, one of the girls wishes to take up that and I will put you in the class with her."

It will be seen that Harry was growing ambitious. He didn't expect to go to college, though nothing would have pleased him better; but he felt that some knowledge of a foreign language could do him no harm. Franklin, whom he had taken as his great exemplar, didn't go to college; yet he made himself one of the foremost scientific men of the age and acquired enduring reputation, not only as a statesman and a patriot, but chiefly as a philosopher.

A little later, Leonard Morgan came round to the desk at which Harry was sitting.

"I brought a Latin grammar with me," he said, "thinking it probable some one might like to begin that language. You can use it until yours comes."

"Thank you," said Harry; and he eagerly took the book, and asked to have a lesson set, which was done.

"I can get more than that," he said.

"How much more?"

"Twice as much."

Still later he recited the double lesson, and so correctly that the teacher's attention was drawn to him.

"That's a smart boy," he said. "I mean to take pains with him. What a pity he can't go to college!"

CHAPTER XVIII
LOST, OR STOLEN

Harry learned rapidly. At the end of four weeks he had completed the Latin grammar, or that part of it which his teacher, thought necessary for a beginner to be familiar with, and commenced translating the easy sentences in "Andrews' Latin Reader."

"You are getting on famously, Harry," said his teacher. "I never had a scholar who advanced so."

"I wish I knew as much as you."

"Don't give me too much credit. When I compare myself with our professors, I feel dissatisfied."

"But you know so much more than I do," said Harry.

"I ought to; I am seven years older."

"What are you going to study, Mr. Morgan?"

"I intend to study law."

"I should like to be an editor," said Harry; "but I don't see much prospect of it."

"Why not?"

"An editor must know a good deal."

"There are some who don't," said Leonard Morgan, with a smile. "However, you would like to do credit to the profession and it is certainly in these modern days a very important profession."

"How can I prepare myself?"

"By doing your best to acquire a good education; not only by study but by reading extensively. An editor should be a man of large information. Have you ever practiced writing compositions?"

"A little; not much."

"If you get time to write anything, and will submit it to me, I will point out such faults as I may notice."

"I should like to do that," said Harry, promptly.

"What subject shall I take?"

"You may choose your own subject. Don't be too ambitious but select something upon which you have some ideas of your own."

"Suppose I take my motto? 'Live and learn.'"

"Do so, by all means. That is a subject upon which you may fairly be said to have some ideas of your own."

In due time Harry presented a composition on this subject. The thoughts were good, but, as might be expected, the expression was somewhat crude, and of course the teacher found errors to correct and suggestions to make. These Harry eagerly welcomed and voluntarily proposed to rewrite the composition. The result was a very much improved draft. He sent a copy home and received in reply a letter from his father, expressing surprise and gratification at the excellence of his essay.

"I am glad, Harry," the letter concluded, "that you have formed just views of the importance of learning. I have never ceased to regret that my own opportunities for education were so limited and that my time has been so much absorbed by the effort to make a living, that I have been able to do so little toward supplying my deficiencies. Even in a pecuniary way an education will open to you a more prosperous career, and lead, I hope, to competence, instead of the narrow poverty which has been my lot. I will not complain of my own want of success, if I can see my children prosper."

But while intent upon cultivating his mind, Harry had not lost sight of the great object which had sent him from home to seek employment among strangers. He had undertaken to meet the note which his father had given Squire Green in payment for the cow. By the first of December he had saved up thirty-three dollars toward this object. By the middle of January the note would come due.

Of course he had not saved so much without the strictest economy, and by denying himself pleasures which were entirely proper. For instance, he was waited upon by Luke Harrison on the first day of December, and asked to join in a grand sleighing excursion to a town ten miles distant, where it was proposed to take supper, and, after a social time, return late in the evening.

"I would like to go," said Harry, who was strongly, tempted, for he was by no means averse to pleasure; "but I am afraid I cannot. How much will it cost?"

"Three dollars apiece. That pays for the supper too."

Harry shook his head. It was for rum a week's wages. If he were not trying to save money for his father, he might have ventured to incur this expense, but he felt that under present circumstances it would not be best.

"I can't go," said Harry.

"Oh, come along," urged Luke. "Don't make such a mope of yourself. You'll be sure to enjoy it."

"I know I should; but I can't afford it."

"I never knew a feller that thought so much of money as you," sneered Luke.

"I suppose it looks so," said Harry; "but it isn't true."

"Everybody says you are a miser."

"I have good reasons for not going."

"If you would come, it would make the expense lighter for the rest of us and you would have a jolly time."

This conversation took place as they were walking home from the store in the evening. Harry pulled out his handkerchief suddenly from his pocket and with it came his pocketbook, containing all his savings. He didn't hear if fall; but Luke did, and the latter, moreover, suspected what it was. He did not call Harry's attention to it, but, falling back, said: "I've got to go back to the store. I forgot something. Good night!"

"Good night!" said Harry, unsuspiciously.

Luke stooped swiftly while our hero's back was turned, and picked up the pocketbook. He slipped it into his own pocket, and, instead of going back to the store, went to his own room, locked the door, and then eagerly pulled out the pocketbook and counted the contents.

"Thirty-three dollars! What a miser that fellow is! It serves him right to lose his money."

CHAPTER XIX
AN UNWELCOME VISITOR

Luke Harrison had picked up Harry's pocketbook, and, though knowing it to be his, concealed the discovery upon the impulse of the moment.

"What I find is mine," he said to himself. "Of course it is. Harry Walton deserves to lose his money."

It will be seen that he had already decided to keep the money. It looked so tempting to him, as his eyes rested on the thick roll of bills--for, though insignificant in amount, the bills were ones and twos, and twenty in number--that he could not make up his mind to return it.

Luke was fond of new clothes. He wanted to reestablish his credit with Merrill, for he was in want of a new coat and knew that it would be useless to order one unless he had some money to pay on account. He decided to use a part of Harry's money for this purpose. It would be better, however, he thought, to wait a day or two, as the news of the loss would undoubtedly spread abroad, and his order might excite suspicion, particularly as he had been in Harry's company at the time the money disappeared. He therefore put the pocketbook into his trunk, and carefully locked it. Then he went to bed.

Meanwhile, Harry reached Mr. Leavitt's unconscious of the serious misfortune which had befallen him. He went into the sitting room and talked a while with Mr. Leavitt, and at ten o'clock took his lamp and went up to bed. While he was undressing he felt in his pocket for his money, intending to lock it up in his trunk as usual. His dismay may be conceived when he could not find it.

Poor Harry sank into a chair with that sudden sinking of the heart which unlooked-for misfortune brings and tried to think where he could have left the pocketbook.

That evening he found himself under the necessity of buying a necktie at the store, and so had taken it from his trunk. Could he have left it on the counter? No; he distinctly remembered replacing it in his pocket. He felt the need of consulting with somebody, and with his lamp in his hand went downstairs again.

"You haven't concluded to sit up all night, have you?" asked Mr. Leavitt, surprised at his reappearance.

"Are you sick, Harry?" asked Mrs. Leavitt. "You're looking dreadfully pale."

"I've lost my pocketbook," said Harry. .

"How much was there in it?" asked his employer.

"Thirty-three dollars," answered Harry.

"Whew! that's a good deal of money to lose. I shouldn't want to lose so much myself. When did you have it last?"

Harry told his story, Mr. Leavitt listening attentively

"And you came right home?"

"Yes."

"Alone."

"No; Luke Harrison came with me."

"Are you two thick together?"

"Not at all. He doesn't like me, and I don't fancy him."

"What was he talking about?"

"He wanted me to join a sleighing party."

"What did you say?"

"I said I couldn't afford it. Then he charged me with being a miser, as he often does."

"Did he come all the way home with you?"

"No; he left me at Deacon Brewster's. He said he must go back to the store."

"There is something queer about this," said Mr. Leavitt, shrewdly. "Do you want my advice?"

"Yes; I wish you would advise me, for I don't know what to do."

"Then go to the store at once. Ask, but without attracting any attention, if Luke came back there after leaving you. Then ask Mr. Meade, the storekeeper, whether he noticed you put back your pocketbook."

"But I know I did."

"Then it will be well to say nothing about it, at least publicly. If you find that Luke's excuse was false, and that he did not go back, go at once to his boarding place, and ask him whether he saw you drop the pocketbook. You might have dropped it and he picked it up."

"Suppose he says no?"

"Then we must watch whether he seems flush of money for the next few days."

This seemed to Harry good advice. He retraced his steps to the store, carefully looking for the lost pocketbook. But of course, it was not to be seen and he entered the store troubled and out of spirits.

"I thought you went home, Harry," said Frank Heath.

"You see I am here again," said our hero.

"Time to shut up shop," said Mr. Meade, the storekeeper. "You boys will have to adjourn till to-morrow."

"Where's Luke Harrison?" asked Frank Heath.

"Didn't he go out with you?"

"Yes; but he left me some time ago. He came back here, didn't he?"

"No; he hasn't been here since."

"He spoke of coming," said Harry. "He wanted me to join that sleighing party."

"Good night, boys," said the storekeeper, significantly.

They took the hint and went out. Their way lay in different directions, and they parted company.

"Now I must call on Luke," said Harry to himself.

"I hope he found the pocketbook. He wouldn't be wicked enough to keep it."

But he was not quite so sure of this as he would like to have been. He felt almost sick as he thought of the possibility that he might never recover the money which he had saved so gladly, though with such painful economy. It represented the entire cash earnings of eleven weeks.

Luke Harrison boarded with a Mr. Glenham, a carpenter, and it was at his door that Harry knocked.

"Is Luke Harrison at home?" he inquired of Mrs. Glenham, who opened the door.

"At home and abed, I reckon," she replied.

"I know it's late, Mrs. Glenham, but it is about a matter of importance that I wish to see Luke."

"I reckon it's about the sleighing party."

"No, it is quite another thing. I won't stay but minute."

"Well, I suppose you can go up."

Harry went upstairs and knocked. Ordinarily, Luke would have been asleep, for generally he sank to sleep five minutes after his head touched the pillow; but to-night the excitement of his dishonest intention kept him awake, and he started uneasily when he heard the knock.

"Who's there?" he called out from the bed.

"It's I--Harry Walton."

"He's come about that pocketbook," thought Luke.

"I'm in bed," he answered.

"I want to see you a minute, on a matter of importance."

"Come to-morrow morning."

"I must see you now."

"Oh, well, come in, if you must," said Luke.

CHAPTER XX

"You seem to be in an awful hurry to see me," said Luke, grumbling. "I was just getting to sleep."

"I've lost my pocketbook. Have you seen it?"

"Have I seen it? That's a strange question. How should I have seen it?"

"I lost it on the way from the store to the house."

"Do you mean to charge me with taking it?"

"I haven't said anything of the sort," said Harry; "but you were with me, and I thought you might have seen it drop out of my pocket."

"Did you drop it out of your pocket?"

"I can't think of any other way I could lose it."

"Of course I haven't seen it. Was that all you woke me up about?"

"Is that all? You talk as if it was a little thing losing thirty-three dollars."

"Thirty-three dollars!" repeated Luke, pretending to be surprised. "You don't mean to say you've lost all that?"

"Yes, I do."

"Well," said Luke, yawning, "I wish I could help you; but I can't. Good night."

"Good night," said Harry, turning away disappointed.

"What success, Harry?" inquired Mr. Leavitt, who had deferred going to bed in order to hear his report.

"None at all," answered Harry.

"Is there anything by which you can identify any of the bills?"

"Yes," answered Harry, with sudden recollection, "I dropped a penful of ink on one of the bills--a two-dollar note--just in the center. I had been writing a letter, and the bill lay on the table near by."

"Good!" said Mr. Leavitt. "Now, supposing Luke has taken this money, how is he likely to spend it?"

"At the tailor's, most likely. He is always talking about new clothes; but lately he hasn't had any because Merrill shut down on him on account of an unpaid bill."

"Then you had better see Merrill and ask him to take particular notice of any bills that Luke pays him."

"Innocence must often be suspected, or guilt would never be detected. It is the only way to get on the track of the missing bills."

Harry saw that this was reasonable and decided to call on Merrill the next day.

"Do you think Luke took it?" asked the tailor.

"I don't know. I don't like to suspect him."

"I haven't much opinion of Luke. He owes me a considerable bill."

"He prefers your clothes to Hayden's, and if he has the money, he will probably come here and spend some of it."

"Suppose he does, what do you want me to do?"

"To examine the bills he pays you, and if you find an ink spot on the center of one let me know."

"I understand. I think I can manage it."

"My money was mostly in ones and twos."

"That may help you. I will bear it in mind."

Two days afterwards, Luke Harrison met Harry.

"Have you found your money, Walton?" he asked.

"No, and I am afraid I never shall," said our hero.

"What do you think has become of it?"

"That's just what I would like to find out," said Harry.

"The only thing you can do is to grin and bear it."

"And be more careful next time."

"Of course."

"He's given it up," said Luke to himself. "I think I can venture to use some of it now. I'll go round to Merrill's and see what he's got in the way of pants."

Accordingly he strolled into Merrill's that evening.

"Got any new cloths in, Merrill?" asked Luke.

"I've got some new cloths for pants."

"That's just what I want."

"You're owing me a bill."

"How much is it?"

"Some over thirty dollars."

"I can't pay it all, but I'll tell you what I'll do. I'll pay you fifteen dollars on account, and you can make me a new pair of pants. Will that answer?"

"All right. Of course I'd rather you'd pay the whole bill. Still I want to be accommodating."

"Let me look at your cloths."

The tailor displayed a variety of cloths, one of which suited Luke's fancy.

"Here's fifteen dollars," he said. "Just credit me with that on the bill, will you?"

"All right," said Merrill.

He proceeded to count the money, which consisted of consisted of ones and twos, and instantly came to the conclusion that it was from Harry's missing pocketbook, particularly as he came upon the identical note with the blot in the center.

Unaware of the manner in which he had betrayed himself, Luke felt quite complacent over his reestablished credit, and that without any expense to himself.

"Have you got any new cloth for coats?" he asked.

"I shall have some new cloths in next week."

"All right. When will you have the pants done?"

"You may call round in two or three days."

"Just make 'em in style, Merrill, and I'll send all my friends here."

"Very well. I hope you'll soon be able to pay me the balance of my bill."

"Oh, yes, to be sure. You won't have to wait long."

He swaggered out of the shop, lighting a cigar.

"My young friend," soliloquized the tailor, watching his exit, "you have walked into my trap neatly. Colman,"--turning to a young man present at the time--"did you see Luke Harrison pay me this money?"

"Yes; to be sure."

"Do you see this blot on one of the bills--a two?"

"Yes; What of it?"

"Nothing. I only called your attention to it."

"I don't see what there is strange about that. Anybody might get ink on a bill, mightn't he?"

"Of course."

Colman was puzzled. He could not understand why he should have been called upon to notice such a trifle; but the tailor had his reasons. He wanted to be able to prove by Colman's testimony that the blotted bill was actually put into his hands by Luke Harrison.

CHAPTER XXI
IN THE TAILOR'S POWER

Is that the bill you spoke of, Walton?" asked the tailor, on Harry's next visit to the shop.

"Yes," said Harry, eagerly. "Where did you get it?"

"You can guess."

"From Luke Harrison?"

"Yes; he paid me, last evening, fifteen dollars on account. This note was among those he paid me."

"It is mine. I can swear to it."

"The rest of the money was yours, no doubt."

"What shall I do, Mr. Merrill?"

"The money is yours, and I will restore it to you after seeing Luke. I will send for him to be here at seven o'clock this evening."

As Luke was at work in his shop that day, the tailor's boy came in with a note. Luke opened it and read as follows:

"Will you call at my shop at seven this evening about the pants you ordered?

"Henry Merrill."

"Tell your father I'll come," said Luke.

At seven o'clock he entered the tailor's shop once more.

"Well, Merrill, what do you want to see me about?" he asked. "Have you cut the pants?"

"No."

"You haven't? I wanted you to go to work on them at once."

"I know; but it was necessary to see you first."

"Why--didn't you take the measure right?"

"Luke," said Mr. Merrill, looking him steadily in the eye, "where did you get that money you paid me?"

"Where did I get the money?" repeated Luke, flushing up. "What makes you ask me that question? Isn't it good money? 'Tisn't counterfeit, is it?"

"I asked you where you got it from?"

"From the man I work for, to be sure," said Luke.

"Will you swear to that?"

"I don't see the use. Can't you take my word?"

"I may as well tell you that Harry Walton recognizes one of the bills as a part of the money he lost."

"He does, does he?" said Luke, boldly. "That's all nonsense. Bills all look alike."

"This one has a drop of ink just in the center. He remembered having dropped a blot upon it."

"What have I to do with that?"

"It is hardly necessary to explain. The evening he lost the money you were with him. Two days after, you pay me one of the bills which he lost," said the tailor.

"Do you mean to say I stole 'em?" demanded Luke.

"It looks like it, unless you can explain how you came by the blotted bill."

"I don't believe I paid you the bill. Very likely it was some one else."

"I thought you would say that, so I called Colman's attention to it. However, if your employer admits paying you the bills, of course you are all right."

Luke remembered very well that he was paid in fives, and that such an appeal would do him no good.

"Does Walton know this?" he asked, sinking into a chair, and wiping the perspiration from his brow.

"Yes; he suspected you."

"I'd like to choke him!" said Luke, fiercely. "The miserly scoundrel!"

"It seems to me he is justified in trying to recover his money. What have you done with the rest of it?"

"Tell me what will be done to me," said Luke, sullenly.

"I didn't steal it. I only picked it up when he dropped it. He deserves to lose it, for being so careless."

"Why didn't you tell him you had found it?"

"I meant to give it to him after a while. I only wanted to keep it long enough to frighten him."

"That was dangerous, particularly as you used it."

"I meant to give him back other money."

"I don't think that excuse will avail you in court."

"Court of justice!" repeated Luke, turning pale.

"He won't have me taken up--will he?"

"He will unless you arrange to restore all the money."

"I've paid you part of it."

"That I shall hand over to him. Have you the rest?"

"I've spent a few dollars. I've got eight dollars left."

"You had better give it to me."

Reluctantly, Luke drew out his pocketbook and passed the eight dollars to Mr. Merrill.

"Now when will you pay the rest?"

"In a few weeks," said Luke.

"That won't do. How much do you earn a week?"

"Fifteen dollars."

"How much do you pay for board?"

"Four dollars."

"Then you will be able to pay eleven dollars at the end of this week."

"I can't get along without money," said Luke.

"You will have to till you pay back the money, unless you prefer appearing before a court of justice."

Luke was just going out when the tailor called him back.

"I believe you owe me thirty dollars. When are you going to pay it?"

"I can't pay it yet a while," said Luke.

"I think you had better," said the tailor quietly.

"I'll pay you as soon as I can."

"You make eleven dollars a week over and above your board and spend it on drink, billiards and fast horses. You are fully able to pay for your clothes promptly and I advise you to do it."

"I'll pay you as soon as I can."

"If you neglect to do it, I may as well tell you that I shall let it be known that you stole Walton's pocketbook."

An expression of alarm overspread Luke's face, and he hastily made the required promise. But he added, "I didn't steal it. I only found it."

"The whole story would be told, and people might think as they pleased. But it is much better for you to avoid all this by paying your bills."

Luke Harrison left the tailor's shop in a very unhappy and disgusted frame of mind.

"If I had the sense to wait till it blew over," he said to himself, "I should have escaped all this: I didn't think Merrill would act so mean. Now I'm in for paying his infernal bill besides. It's too bad."

Just then he came upon Frank Heath, who hailed him.

"Luke, come and play a game of billiards."

"If you'll promise not to beat me. I haven't got a cent of money."

"You haven't? What have you done with those bills you had this afternoon?"

"I've paid 'em over to Merrill," said Luke, hesitating.

"He was in a deuced stew about his bill."

"When are your pants going to be ready?"

"I don't know," said Luke, with a pang of sorrow.

"Merrill's making them, isn't he?"

"He says he won't till I pay the whole bill."

"Seems to me your credit ain't very good, Luke."

"It's good enough, be he's hard up for money. I guess he's going to fail. If you'll lend me a couple of dollars, I'll go around and have a game."

Frank Heath laughed.

"You'll have to go to some one else, Luke," he said.

Luke passed a disagreeable evening. Cut off by his want of money from his ordinary amusements, and depressed by the thought that things would be no better till he had paid his bills, he lounged about, feeling that he was a victim of ill luck. It did not occur to him that that ill luck was of his own bringing.

CHAPTER XXII
THE COMING OF THE MAGICIAN

The week passed and Luke carefully avoided our hero going so far as to cross the street so as not to meet him. On Saturday evening, according to his arrangement, Luke was to have paid the surplus of his wages, after meeting his board bill, to Mr. Merrill, for Harry.

But he did not go near him. On Monday, the tailor meeting him, inquired why he had not kept his agreement.

"The fact is," said Luke, "I have been unlucky."

"How unlucky?"

"I had my wages loose in my pocket, and managed to lose them somehow."

"That is very singular," said the tailor, suspiciously.

"Why is it singular?" asked Luke. "Didn't Harry Walton lose his money?"

"You seem to have lost yours at a very convenient time."

"It's hard on me," said Luke. "Owing so much, I want to pay as quick as I can, so as to have my wages to myself. Don't you see that?"

"Where do you think you lost the money?"

"I'm sure I don't know," said Luke.

"Well," said Merrill, dryly, "I hope you will take better care of your wages next Saturday evening."

"I mean to. I can't afford to lose anymore."

"I don't believe, a word of what he says about losing his money," said the tailor, privately, to Harry. "I think it's only a trick to get rid of paying you."

"Don't you think he'll pay me?" asked Harry.

"He won't if he can help it," was the answer. "He's a slippery customer. I believe his money is in his pocket at this moment."

Mr. Merrill was not quite right; but it was only as to the whereabouts of the money. It was in Luke's trunk. He intended to run away, leaving all his creditors in the lurch. This was the "new way to pay old debts," which occurred to Luke as much the easiest.

The next Saturday evening, Mr. Merrill waited in vain for a call from his debtor.

"What excuse will he have now?" he thought.

On Monday morning he learned that Luke had left town without acquainting anyone with his destination. It transpired, also, that he was owing at his boarding house for two weeks' board. He was thus enabled to depart with nearly thirty dollars, for parts unknown.

"He's a hard case," said Mr. Merrill to Harry. "I am afraid he means to owe us for a long time to come."

"Where do you think he is gone?" asked Harry.

"I have no idea. He has evidently been saving up money to help him out of town. Sometime we may get upon his track, and compel him to pay up."

"That won't do me much good," said Harry, despondently. And then he told the tailor why he wanted the money. "Now," he concluded, "I shan't be able to have the money ready in time."

"You'll have most of it ready, won't you?"

"I think I will."

"I would lend you the money myself," said the tailor, "but I've got a heavy payment to meet and some of my customers are slow pay, though I have not many as bad as Luke Harrison."

"Thank you, Mr. Merrill," said Harry. "I am as much obliged to you as if you could lend the money."

But it is said that misfortunes never come singly. The very next day Mr. Leavitt received a message from the wholesale dealer to whom he sold his shoes, that the market was glutted and sales slow.

"I shall not want any more goods for a month or two," the letter concluded. "I will let you know, when I more."

Mr. Leavitt read this letter aloud in the shop.

"So it seems we are to have a vacation," he said. "That's the worst of the shoe trade. It isn't steady. When it's good everybody rushes into it, and the market soon gets overstocked. Then there's no work for weeks."

This was a catastrophe for which Harry was no prepared. He heard the announcement with a grave face, for to him it was a serious calamity. Twenty-three dollars were all that he had saved from the money lost and this would be increased by a dollar or two only, when he had settled up with Mr. Leavitt. If he stayed here did not obtain work, he must pay his board, and that would soon swallow up his money. Could he get work in any other shop? That was an important question.

"Do you think I can get into any other shop in town?" he inquired anxiously of Mr. Leavitt.

"You can try, Harry; but I guess you'll find others no better off than I."

This was not very encouraging, but Harry determined not to give up without an effort. He devoted the next day to going around among the shoe shops; but everywhere he met with unfavorable answers. Some had ready suspended. Others were about to do so.

"It seems as if all my money must go," thought Harry, looking despondently at his little hoard. "First the ten dollars Luke Harrison stole. Then work stopped. I don't know but it would be better for me to go home."

But the more Harry thought of this, the less he liked it. It would be an inglorious ending to his campaign. Probably now he would not be able to carry out his plan of paying for the cow; but if his father should lose it, he might be able, if he found work, to buy him another Squire Green's cow was not the only cow in the world and all would not be lost if he could not buy her.

"I won't give up yet," said Harry, pluckily. "I must expect to meet with some bad luck. I suppose everybody does. Something'll turn up for me if I try to make it."

This was good philosophy. Waiting passively for something to turn up is bad policy and likely to lead to disappointment; but waiting actively, ready to seize any chance that may offer, is quite different. The world is full of chances, and from such chances so seized has been based many a prosperous career.

During his first idle day, Harry's attention was drawn to a handbill which had been posted up in the store, the post office, the tavern, and other public places in the village. It was to this effect:

"PROFESSOR HENDERSON,

"The celebrated Magician,

"Will exhibit his wonderful feats of Magic and Sleight of Hand in the Town Hall this evening, commencing at 8 o'clock. In the course of the entertainment he will amuse the audience by his wonderful exhibition of Ventriloquism, in which he is unsurpassed.

"Tickets 25 cents. Children under twelve, 15 cents."

In a country village, where amusements are few, such entertainments occupy a far more important place than in a city, where amusements abound.

"Are you going to the exhibition, Walton?" asked Frank Heath.

"I don't know," said Harry.

"Better come. It'll be worth seeing."

In spite of his economy, our hero wanted to go.

"The professor's stopping at the tavern. Come over, and we may see him," said Frank.

CHAPTER XXIII
THE VENTRILOQUIST

The boys went into the public room of the tavern. In the center was a stove, around which were gathered a miscellaneous crowd, who had assembled, as usual, to hear and talk over the news of the day. At the farther end of the room was a bar, where liquor and cigars were sold. The walls of the room, which was rather low-studded, were ornamented by sundry notices and posters of different colors, with here and there an engraving of no great artistic excellence--one representing a horse race, another a steamer of the Cunard Line, and still another, the Presidents of the United States grouped together, with Washington as the central figure.

"Have a cigar, Walton?" asked Frank Heath.

"No, thank you, Frank."

"You haven't got so far along, hey?"

"I don't think it would do me any good," said Harry.

"Maybe not; but jolly comfortable on a cold night. The worst of it is, it's mighty expensive."

Frank walked up to the bar and bought a ten-cent cigar. He returned and sat down on a settee.

"The magician isn't here," said Harry.

"Hush, he is here!" said Frank, in a low voice, as the door opened, and a tall, portly man entered the room.

Professor Henderson--for it was he--walked up the bar, and followed Frank Heath's example in the purchase of a cigar Then he glanced leisurely round the apartment. Apparently, his attention was fixed by our hero, for he walked up to him, and said: "Young man, I would like to speak to you."

"All right, sir," said Harry, in surprise.

"If you are not otherwise occupied, will you accompany me to my room?"

"Certainly, sir," returned Harry, in fresh wonder.

"Perhaps he's going to take in Walton as partner," Frank Heath suggested to Tom Frisbie.

"I wonder what he want anyway?" said Frisbie. "Why didn't he take you?"

"Because I'm too sharp," said Frank. "I should see through his tricks."

Meanwhile, Harry had entered the professor's chamber.

"Sit down," said the magician. "I'll tell you what I want of you. I want you to take tickets at the door of hall to-night. Can you do it?"

"Yes, sir," said Harry, promptly.

"It seems easy enough," said the professor; "but not everyone can do it rapidly without making mistakes. Are you quick at figures?"

"I am usually considered so," said our hero.

"I won't ask whether you are honest, for you would so, of course."

"I hope--" commenced Harry.

"I know what you are going to say; but there is no need of saying it," interrupted the magician. "I judge from your face, which is an honest one. I have traveled about a good deal, and I am a good judge of faces."

"You shall not be disappointed, sir."

"I know that, in advance. Now, tell me if you are at work, or do you attend school?"

"I have been at work in a shoe shop in this village, sir."

"Not now?"

"No, sir; business is dull, and work has given out."

"What are you going to do next?"

"Anything by which I can earn an honest living."

"That's the way to talk. I'll take you into my employ, if you have no objection to travel."

Objection to travel! Who ever heard of a boy of fifteen who had an objection to travel?

"But will your parents consent? That is the next question. I don't want to entice any boys away from home against their parents' consent."

"My parents do not live here. They live farther north, in the town of Granton."

"Granton? I never was there. Is it a large place?"

"No, sir, it is a very small place. My father consented to have me leave home and he will have no objection to my earning my living in any honest way."

"Well, my young friend, I can assure you that my way is an honest one, though I frankly confess I do my best to deceive the people who come to my entertainments."

"What is it you want me to do, sir?"

"Partly what you are going to do to-night--take tickets at the door; but that is not all. I have to carry about considerable apparatus and I need help about arranging it. Sometimes, also, I need help in my experiments. I had a young man with me; but he is taken down with a fever and obliged to go home. It is not likely, as his health is delicate, that he will care to resume his position. I must have somebody in his place. I have no doubt you will answer my purpose."

"How much pay do you give, sir?"

"A practical question," said the professor, smiling.

"To begin with, of course I pay traveling expenses, and I can offer you five dollars a week besides. Will that be satisfactory?"

"Yes, sir," said Harry, his heart giving a great throb of exultation as he realized that his new business would give him two dollars week more than his work in the shop, besides being a good deal more agreeable, since it would give him a chance to see a little of the world.

"Can you start with me to-morrow morning?"

"Yes, sir."

"Then it is settled. But it is time you were at the hall. I will give you a supply of small bills and, change, as you may have to change some bills."

He drew from his side pocket a wallet, which he placed in the hands of our hero.

"This wallet contains twenty dollars," he said: "Of course you will bring me back that amount, in addition to what you take at the door this evening."

"Very well, sir."

"You can wait for me at the close of the evening, and hand me all together.

Now go over to the hall, as the doors are to be open at half past seven o'clock."

When Frank Heath and his companion went over to the Town Hall they found Harry making change.

"Hello, Walton!" said Frank. "Are you the treasurer of this concern?"

"It seems so," said Harry.

"You'll let in your friends for nothing, won't you?"

"Not much. I charge them double price."

"Well here's our money. I say, Tom, I wonder the old fellow didn't take me instead of Walton."

"That's easily told. You don't look honest enough."

"Oh, if it comes to that, he passed over you, too, Tom."

"He wouldn't insult a gentleman of my dignity. Come on; there's room on the front seat."

Harry was kept busy till ten minutes after eight. By that time about all who intended to be present were in the hall and the magician was gratified by seeing that it was crowded. He was already well known in the village, having been in the habit of visiting it every for years and his reputation for dexterity, and especially for ventriloquism, had called out this large audience.

The professor's tricks excited great wonder in the younger spectators. I will only dwell slightly on his ventriloquism. When he came to this part of the entertainment, he said: "Will any young gentleman assist me?"

Frank Heath immediately left his seat and took up his position beside the professor.

"Now, sir," said the professor, "I want to ask you a question or two. Will you answer me truly?"

A gruff voice appeared to proceed from Frank's mouth, saying: "Yes, sir."

"Are you married, sir?"

Again the same gruff voice answered: "Yes, sir; I wish I wasn't;" to the great delight of the small boys.

"Indeed, sir! I hope your wife doesn't make it uncomfortable for you."

"She licks me," Frank appeared to answer.

"I am sorry. What does she lick you with?"

"With a broomstick."

Frank looked foolish and there was a general laugh.

"I hope she doesn't treat you so badly very often, sir."

"Yes, she does, every day," was the answer. "If she knowed I was up here telling you, she'd beat me awful."

"In that case, sir, I won't be cruel enough to keep you here any longer. Take my advice, sir, and get a divorce."

"So I will, by hokey!"

And Frank, amid hearty laughter, resumed his seat, not having uttered a word, the professor being responsible for the whole conversation.

CHAPTER XXIV
HARRY'S LETTER

During Harry's absence, the little household at Granton had got along about as usual. They lived from hand to mouth. It required sharp financiering to provide food and clothes for the little family.

There was one neighbor who watched their progress sharply and this was Squire Green. It will be remembered that he had bound Mr. Walton to forfeit ten dollars, if, at the end of six months, he was not prepared to pay the forty dollars and interest which he had agreed to pay for the cow. It is a proof of the man's intense meanness that, though rich while his neighbor was poor, he was strongly in hopes that the latter would incur the forfeit and be compelled to pay it.

One morning Squire Green accosted Mr. Walton, the squire being at work in his own front yard.

"Good morning, neighbor Walton," he said.

"Good morning, squire."

"How is that cow a-doin'?"

"Pretty well."

"She's a good cow."

"Not so good as the one I lost."

"You're jokin' now, neighbor. It was my best cow. I wouldn't have sold her except to obleege."

"She doesn't give as much milk as my old one."

"Sho! I guess you don't feed her as well as I did."

"She fares just as well as the other one did. Of course, I don't know how you fed her."

"She allers had her fill when she was with me. Le' me see, how long is it since

I sold her to ye?"

Though the squire apparently asked for information, he knew the time to a day and was not likely to forget.

"It's between four and five months, I believe."

"Jus'so. You was to be ready to pay up at the end of six months."

"That was the agreement."

"You'd better be a-savin' up for it."

"There isn't much chance of my saving. It's all I can do to make both ends meet."

"You don't say so," said the squire, secretly pleased.

"My farm is small and poor, and doesn't yield much."

"But you work out, don't you?"

"When I get a chance. You don't want any help, do you, squire? I might work off part of the debt that way."

"Mebbe next spring I'd like some help."

"That will be too late to meet my note, unless you'll renew."

"I'll see about it," said the squire, evasively. "What do you hear from that boy of yours? Is he doin' well?"

"He's at work in a shoe shop."

"Does it pay well?"

"He doesn't get much just at first."

"Then he won't be able to pay for the cow," thought the squire. "That's what I wanted to know."

"He'd better have gone to work for me," he said

"No, I think he will do better away from home. He will get a good trade that he can fall back upon hereafter, even if he follows some other business."

"Wal, I never learned no trade but I've got along middlin' well," said the squire, in a complacent tone. "Farmin's good enough for me."

"I would say the same if I had your farm, squire. You wouldn't exchange, would you?"

"That's a good joke, neighbor Walton. When I make up my mind to do it. I'll let you know."

"What a mean old curmudgeon he is!" thought Hiram Walton, as he kept on his way to the village store. "He evidently intends to keep me to my agreement and will exact the ten dollars in case I can't pay for the cow at the appointed time. It will be nothing but a robbery."

This was not the day for a letter from Harry but it occurred to Mr. Walton to call at the post office. Contrary to his anticipations, a letter was handed him.

"I won't open it till I get home," he said to himself.

"I've got a letter from Harry," he said, as he entered the house.

"A letter from Harry? It isn't his day for writing," said Mrs. Walton. "What does he say?"

"I haven't opened the letter yet. Here, Tom, open and read it aloud."

Tom opened the letter and read as follows:

"Dear Father:--I must tell you, to begin with, that I have been compelled to stop work in the shoe shop. The market is overstocked and trade has become very dull.

"Of course, I felt quite bad when Mr. Leavitt told me this, for I feared it would prevent my helping you pay for the cow, as I want so much to do. I went round to several other shops, hoping to get in, but I found it impossible. Still, I have succeeded in getting something to do that will pay me better than work in the shop. If you were to guess all day, I don't believe you would guess what business it is. So, to relieve your suspense, I will tell you that I have engaged as assistant to Professor Henderson, the famous magician and ventriloquist and am to start to-morrow on a tour with him."

"Assistant to a magician!" exclaimed Mrs. Walton

"What does the boy know about magic?"

"It's a bully business," said Tom, enthusiastically. "I only wish I was in Harry's shoes. I'd like to travel round with a magician first-rate."

"You're too thick-headed, Tom," said Marry.

"Shut up!" said Tom. "I guess I'm as smart as you, any day."

"Be quiet, both of you!" said Mr. Walton. "Now, Tom, go on with your brother's letter."

Tom proceeded: "I am to take money at the door. We are going about in the southern part of the State and shall visit some towns in Massachusetts, the professor says. You know I've never been round any and I shall like traveling and seeing new places. Professor Henderson is very kind and I think I shall like him. He pays my traveling expenses and five dollars a week, which is nearly twice as much money as I got from Mr. Leavitt. I can't help thinking I am lucky in getting so good a chance only a day after I lost my place in the shoe shop. I hope, yet, to be able to pay for the cow when the money comes due.

"Love to all at home.

"Harry."

"Harry's lucky," said Mary. "He can get along."

"He is fortunate to find employment at once," said his father; "though something which he can follow steadily is better. But the pay is good and I am glad he has it."

"How long it seems since Harry was at home," said his mother. "I wish I could see him."

"Yes, it would be pleasant," said Mr. Walton; "but the boy has his own way to make, so we will be thankful that he is succeeding so well."

CHAPTER XXV
A STRANGE COMPANION

At ten o'clock the next day, Harry presented himself at the hotel. He carried in his hand a carpetbag lent him by Mr. Leavitt, which contained his small stock of under-clothing. His outside suits he left at Mr. Leavitt's, not wishing to be encumbered with them while traveling.

"I see you are on time," said the professor.

"Yes, sir; I always mean to be."

"That's well; now if you'll jump into my buggy with me, we will ride round to the Town Hall and take in my apparatus. I have to keep a carriage," said the magician, as they rode along. "It saves me a great deal of trouble by making me independent of cars and stages."

The apparatus was transferred to a trunk in the back part of the buggy and securely locked.

"Now we are all ready," said Professor Henderson,

"Would you like to drive?"

"Yes, sir," answered Harry, with alacrity.

"I am going to give an entertainment in Holston this evening," said his new employer. "Were you ever there?"

"No, sir."

"It is a smart little place and although the population is not large, I always draw a full house."

"How far is it, sir?"

"About six miles."

Harry was sorry it was not farther, as he enjoyed driving. His companion leaned back at his ease and talked on various subjects. He paused a moment and Harry was startled by hearing a stifled child's voice just behind him: "Oh, let me out! Don't keep me locked up here!"

The reins nearly fell from his hands. He turned and heard the voice apparently proceeding from the trunk.

"What's the matter?" asked Professor Henderson.

"I thought I heard a child's voice."

"So you did," said the voice again.

The truth flashed upon Harry. His companion was exerting some of his powers as a ventriloquist.

"Oh, it is you, sir," he said, smiling.

His companion smiled.

"You are right," he said.

"I don't see how you can do it," said Harry.

"Practice, my boy."

"But practice wouldn't make everybody a ventriloquist, would it?"

"Most persons might become ventriloquists, though in an unequal degree. I often amuse myself by making use of it for playing practical jokes upon people.

"Do you see that old lady ahead?"

"Yes, sir."

"I'll offer her a ride. If she accepts, you'll see sport. I shall make you talk but you must be careful to say nothing yourself."

A few rods farther on, they overtook an old woman.

"Good morning, ma'am" said the professor. "Won't you get in and ride? It's easier riding than walking."

The old women scanned his countenance and answered: "Thank you, sir, I'm obleeged to ye. I don't mind if I do."

She was assisted into the carriage and sat at one end of the seat, Harry being in the middle.

"I was going to see my darter, Nancy," said the old women. "Mrs. Nehemiah Babcock her name is. Mebbe you know her husband."

"I don't think I do," said the professor.

"He's got a brother in Boston in the dry goods business. Mebbe you've been at his store."

"Mebbe I have."

"I ginerally call to see my darter--her name is Nancy--once a week; but it's rather hard for me to walk, now I'm gettin' on in years."

"You're most eighty, ain't you?" appeared to proceed from Harry's mouth. Our hero's face twitched and he had hard work to keep from laughing.

"Indeed, I'm not!" said the old lady, indignantly.

"I'm only sixty-seven and folks say I don't look more'n sixty," and the old lady looked angrily at Harry.

"You must excuse him, ma'am," said the professor, soothingly. "He is no judge of a lady's age."

"I should think not, indeed."

"Indeed, madam, you are very young looking."

The old lady was pacified by this compliment but looked askance at Harry.

"Is he your son?"

"No, ma'am."

The old lady sniffed, as if to say, "So much the better for you."

"Are you travelin' far?" asked the old lady.

"What do you want to know for?" Harry appeared to ask.

"You're a sassy boy!" exclaimed the old woman.

"Harry," said Professor Henderson, gravely, "how often have I told you not to be so unmannerly?"

"He orter be whipped," said the old lady. "Ef I had a boy that was so sassy, I'd larn him manners!"

"I'm glad I ain't your boy," Harry appeared to reply.

"I declare I won't ride another step if you let him insult me so," said the old woman, glaring at our hero.

Professor Henderson caught her eye and significantly touched his forehead, giving her to understand that Harry was only "half-witted."

"You don't say so" she ejaculated, taking the hint at once. "How long's he been so?"

"Ever since he was born."

"Ain't you afraid to have him drive?"

"Oh, not at all. He understands horses as well as I do."

"What's his name?"

Before the professor's answer could be heard, Harry appeared to rattle off the extraordinary name: "George Washington Harry Jefferson Ebenezer Popkins."

"My gracious! Has he got all them names?"

"Why not? What have you got to say about it, old women?" said the same voice.

"Oh, I ain't got no objection," said the old woman.

"You may have fifty-'leven names ef you want to."

"I don't interfere with his names," said the professor.

"If he chooses to call himself--"

"George Washington Harry Jefferson Ebenezer Popkins," repeated the voice, with great volubility.

"If he chooses to call himself by all those names, I'm sure I don't care. How far do you go, ma'am?"

"About quarter of a mile farther."

The professor saw that he must proceed to his final joke.

"Let me out! Don't keep me locked up here!" said the child's voice, from behind, in a pleading tone.

"What's that?" asked the startled old lady.

"What's what?" asked the professor, innocently.

"That child that wants to get out."

"You must have dreamed it, my good lady."

"No, there 'tis agin'," said the old lady, excited.

"It's in the trunk behind you," said the assumed voice, appearing to proceed from our hero.

"So 'tis," said the old lady, turning halfway round.

"Oh, I shall die! Let me out! Let me out!"

"He's locked up his little girl in the trunk," Harry seemed to say.

"You wicked man, let her out this minute," said the old lady, very much excited. "Don't you know no better than to lock up a child where she can't get no air?"

"There is no child in the trunk, I assure you," said Professor Henderson, politely.

"Don't you believe him," said Harry's voice.

"Do let me out, father!" implored the child's voice

"If you don't open the trunk, I'll have you took up for murder," said the old lady.

"I will open it to show you are mistaken."

The professor got over the seat, and, opening the trunk, displayed its contents to the astonished old lady.

"I told you that there was no child there," he said; "but you would not believe me."

"Le' me out," gasped the old woman. "I'd rather walk. I never heerd of such strange goin's on afore."

"If you insist upon it, madam, but I'm sorry to lose your company. Take this with you and read it."

He handed her one of his bills, which she put in her pocket, saying she couldn't see to read it.

When they were far enough off to make it safe, Harry gave vent to his mirth, which he had restrained till this at difficulty and laughed long and loud.

CHAPTER XXVI
PAGES FROM THE PAST

W hat will the old lady think of you?" said Harry.

"She will have a very bad opinion till she puts on her specs and read the bill. That will explain all. I shouldn't be surprised to see her at my entertainment."

"I wonder if she'll recognize me," said Harry.

"No doubt; as soon as she learns with whom she rode, she'll be very curious to come and see me perform."

"How old were you when you began to be a ventriloquist?"

"I was eighteen. I accidentally made the discovery, and devoted considerable time to perfecting myself in it before acquainting anyone with it. That idea came later. You see when I was twenty-one, with a little property which I inherited from my uncle, I went into business for myself; but I was young and inexperienced in management, and the consequence was, that in about two years I failed. I found it difficult to get employment as a clerk, business being very dull at the time. While uncertain what to do, one of my friends, to whom I had communicated my power, induced me to give me a public entertainment, combining with it a few tricks of magic, which I had been able to pick up from books. I succeeded so well my vocation in life became Professor Henderson."

"It must be great fun to be a ventriloquist."

"So I regarded it at first. It may not be a very high vocation but I make the people laugh and so I regard myself as a public benefactor. Indeed, I once did an essential service to a young man by means of my ventriloquism."

"I should like very much to hear the story."

"I will tell you. One day, a young man, a stranger, came to me and introduced himself under the name of Paul Dabney. He said that I might, if I would, do him a great service. His father had died the year previous, leaving a farm and other property to the value of fifteen thousand dollars. Of course, being as only son, he expected that this would be left to himself, or, at least, the greater part of it. Conceive his surprise, therefore, when the will came to be read, to find that the entire property was left to his Uncle Jonas, his father brother, who, for three years past, had been a member of the family. Jonas had never prospered in life, and his brother, out of pity, had offered him an asylum on his farm. He had formerly been a bookkeeper and was an accomplished penman.

"The will was so extraordinary--since Paul and his father had always been on perfectly good terms--that the young man was thunderstruck. His uncle expressed hypocritical surprise at the nature of the will.

"'I don't believe my father made that will,' exclaimed Paul, angrily.

"'What do you mean by that?' demanded the uncle.

"His anger made Paul think that he had hit upon the truth, particularly as his uncle was an adroit penman.

"He carefully examined the will; but the writing so closely resembled his father's that he could see no difference. The witnesses were his Uncle Jonas and a hired man, who, shortly after witnessing the signature, had been discharged and had disappeared from the neighborhood. All this excited Paul's suspicions.

"His uncle offered him a home on the farm; but positively refused to give him any portion of the property.

"'I sympathize with you,' I said at the conclusion of Paul's story; 'but how can I help you?'

"'I will tell you, sir,' he replied. 'You must know that my Uncle Jonas is very superstitious. I mean, through your help, to play upon his fears and thus induce him to give up the property to me.'

"With this he unfolded his plan and I agreed to help him. His uncle lived ten miles distant. I procured a laborer's disguise and the morning after--Paul having previously gone back--I entered the yard of the farmhouse. The old man was standing outside, smoking a pipe.

"'Can you give me work?' I asked.

"'What kind of work?' inquired Jonas.

"'Farm work,' I answered.

"'How much do you want?'

"'Eight dollars a month.'

"'I'll give you six,' he said.

"'That's too little.'

"'It's the most I'll give you.'

"'Then I'll take,' I replied, and was at once engaged.

"Delighted to get me so cheap, the sordid old man asked me no troublesome questions. I knew enough of farm work to get along pretty well and not betray myself.

"That night I concealed myself in the old man's apartment without arousing his suspicions, Paul helping me. After he had been in bed about twenty minutes, I thought it time to begin. Accordingly I uttered a hollow groan.

"'Eh! What's that?' cried the old man, rising in bed.

"'I am the spirit of your dead brother,' I answered, throwing my voice near the bed.

"'What do you want?' he asked, his teeth chattering.

"'You have cheated Paul out of his property.'

"'Forgive me!' he cried, terror-stricken.

"'Then give him back the property.'

"'The whole?' he groaned.

"'Yes, the whole.'

"'Are--are you really my brother?'

"'I will give you this proof. Unless you do as I order you, in three days you will be with me.'

"'What, dead?' he said, shuddering.

"'Yes,' I answered in sepulchral a tone as possible.

"'Are--are you sure of it?'

"'If you doubt it, disobey me.'

"'I'll do it, but--don't come again.'

"'Be sure you do it then.'

"I ceased to speak, being tired, and escaped as soon as I could. But the battle was not yet over. The next day gave Jonas courage. Afternoon came and he had done nothing. He was with me in the field when I threw a hollow voice, which seemed to be close to his ear. I said, 'Obey, or in three days you die.'

"He turned pale as a sheet and asked me if I heard anything. I expressed surprise and this confirmed him in his belief of the ghostly visitation. He went to the house, sent for a lawyer and transferred the entire property to his nephew. The latter made him a present of a thousand dollars and so the affair ended happily. Paul paid me handsomely for my share in the trick and the next day I made an excuse for leaving the farm."

"Did the old man ever discover your agency in the affair, Professor Henderson?"

"Never. He is dead now and my friend Paul is happily married, and has a fine family. His oldest boy is named after me. But here we are in Holston."

CHAPTER XXVII
A MYSTIFYING PERFORMANCE

The people of Holston turned out in large numbers. Among the first to appear was the old lady whom the professor had taken up on his way over. "You're the boy that was so sassy to me this mornin'," she said, peering at Harry through her spectacles.

"I didn't say a word to you," said Harry.

"I'm afraid you're tellin' fibs. I heerd you."

"It was the professor. He put the words in my mouth."

"Well, come to think on't the voice was different from yours. Then there wa'n't nobody in the trunk?"

"No, ma'am," said Harry, smiling.

"It's wonderful, I declare for't. This is my darter, Mrs. Nehemiah Babcock," continued the old lady. "Nancy, this is the ventriloquer's boy. I thought he was sassy to me this mornin'; but he says he didn't speak a word. How much is to pay?" said the old lady.

"I won't charge you anything," said Harry. "Professor Henderson told me, if you came to let you in free, and any of your family."

"Really, now, that's very perlite of the professor," said the old lady. "He's a gentleman if ever there was one. Do you hear, Nancy, we can go in without payin' a cent. That's all on, account of your marm's being acquainted with the professor. I'm glad I come."

The old lady and her party entered the hall, and being early, secured good seats. Tom, her grandson, was glad to be so near, as he was ambitious to assist the professor in case volunteers were called for.

"Will any young gentleman come forward and assist me in the next trick?"

asked the professor, after a while.

Tom started from his seat. His grandmother tried to seize him by the coat but he was too quick for her.

"Oh, let him go," said his mother. "He won't come to any harm."

"Is this your first appearance as a magician?" asked the professor.

"Yes, sir," answered Tom, with a grin.

"Very good. I will get you to help me, but you mustn't tell anybody how the tricks are done."

"No, sir, I won't."

"As I am going trust you with a little money, I want to ask you whether you are strictly honest."

"Yes, sir."

"I am glad to hear it. Do you see this piece of gold?"

"Yes, sir."

"What is its value?"

"Ten dollars," answered Tom, inspecting it.

"Very good. I want you hold it for me. I give you warning that I mean to make it pass out of you hand."

"I don't think you can do it, sir."

"Well, perhaps not. You look like a pretty sharp customer. It won't be easy to fool you."

"You bet."

"Nancy," whispered the old lady to her daughter. "I hope you don't allow Tom to talk so."

"Look, mother, see want he's going to do."

"What I propose to do," said the professor, "is to make that coin pass into the box on the table. I may not be able to do it, as the young gentleman is on his guard. However, I will try. Presto, change!"

"It didn't go," said Tom. "I've got it here."

"Have you? Suppose you open your hand."

Tom opened his hand.

"Well, what have you got? Is it the gold piece?"

"No sir," said Tom, astonished; "it's a cent."

"Then, sir, all I can say is, you have treated me badly. In order to prevent my getting the gold piece into the box, you changed it into a cent."

"No, I didn't," said Tom.

"Then perhaps I have succeeded, after all. The fact is, I took out the gold piece and put a penny in its place, so that you might not know the difference. Now here is the key of that box. Will you unlock it?"

Tom unlocked it, only to find another box inside. In fact, it was a perfect nest of boxes. In the very last of all was found the gold coin.

"It's very strange you didn't feel it go out of your hand," said the professor.

"I am afraid you are not quick enough to make a magician. Can you fire a pistol?"

"Yes, sir," said Tom.

"Will any lady lend me a ring?" asked the professor.

One was soon found

"I will load the pistol," said the professor, "and put the ring in with the rest of the charge. It appears to be rather too large. I shall have to hammer it down."

He brought down a hammer heavily upon the ring and soon bent it sufficiently to get it into the pistol.

"Now, sir," he said, "take the pistol, and stand off there. All right, sir. When I give the word, I want you to fire. One, two, three!"

Tom fired, his grandmother uttering a half suppressed shriek at the report. When the smoke cleared away, the professor was holding the ring between his thumb and finger, quite uninjured.

Professor Henderson's attention had been drawn to his companion of the morning. He observed that she had taken off her bonnet. He went up to her, and said, politely, "Madam, will you kindly lend me your bonnet?"

"Massy sakes, what do you want of it?"

"I won't injure it, I assure you."

"You may take it, ef you want to," said the old lady; "but be keerful and don't bend it."

"I will be very careful; but, madam," he said, in seeming surprise, "what have you got in it?"

"Nothing, sir."

"You are mistaken. See there, and there, and there"; and he rapidly drew out three onions, four turnips, and a couple of potatoes. "Really, you must have thought you were going to market."

"They ain't mine," gasped the old lady.

"Then it's very strange how they got into your bonnet. And--let me see--here's an egg, too."

"I never see sich doin's."

"Granny, I guess a hen made her nest in your bonnet," whispered Tom.

The old lady shook her head in helpless amazement.

CHAPTER XXVIII
AN UNEXPECTED PAYMENT

A week later Harry reached a brisk manufacturing place which I will call Centreville. He assisted the professor during the afternoon to get ready the hall for his evening performance and, at half past five, took his seat at the supper table in the village hotel.

Just as Harry began to eat, he lifted his eyes, and started in surprise as he recognized, in his opposite neighbor, Luke Harrison, whose abrupt departure without paying his debts the reader will remember. Under the circumstances, it will not be wondered at that our hero's look was not exactly cordial. As for Luke, he was disagreeably startled at Harry's sudden appearance. Not knowing his connection with Professor Henderson, he fancied that our hero was in quest of him and not being skilled in the law, felt a little apprehension as to what course he might take. It was best, he concluded to conciliate him.

"How are you, Walton?" he said.

"I am well," said Harry, coldly.

"How do you happen to be in this neighborhood?"

"On business," said Harry, briefly.

Luke jumped to the conclusion that the business related to him and, conscious of wrong-doing, felt disturbed.

"I'm glad to see you," he said. "It seems pleasant to see an old acquaintance"--he intended to say "friend."

"You left us rather suddenly," said Harry.

"Why, yes," said Luke, hesitating. "I had reasons. I'll tell you about it after supper."

As Harry rose from the table, Luke joined him.

"Come upstairs to my room, Walton," he said, "and have a cigar."

"I'll go upstairs with you; but I don't smoke."

"You'd better learn. It's a great comfort."

"Do you board here?"

"Yes. I found I shouldn't have to pay any more than at a boarding house and the grub's better. Here's my room. Walk in."

He led the way into a small apartment on the top floor.

"This is my den," he said. "There isn't but one chair; but I'll sit on the bed. When did you reach town?"

"About noon"

"Are you going to stop long?" asked Luke.

"I shall stay here till I get through with my errand," answered Harry, shrewdly; for he saw what Luke thought, and it occurred to him that he might turn it to advantage.

Luke looked a little uneasy.

"By the way, Walton," he said, "I believe I owe you a little money."

"Yes. I believe so."

"I'm sorry I can't pay you the whole of it. It costs considerable to live, you know; but I'll pay part."

"Here are five dollars," he said. "I'll pay you the rest as soon as I can--in a week or two."

Harry took the bank note with secret self-congratulation, for he had given up the debt as bad, and never expected to realize a cent of it.

"I am glad to get it," he said. "I have a use for all my money. Are you working in this town?"

"Yes. The shoe business is carried on here considerably. Are you still working for Mr. Leavitt?"

"No; I've left him."

"What are you doing, then?"

"I'm traveling with Professor Henderson."

"What, the magician?"

"Yes."

"And is that what brought you to Centreville?"

"Yes."

Luke whistled.

"I thought--" he began.

"What did you think?"

"I thought," answered Luke, evasively, "that you might be looking for work in some of the shoe shops here."

"Is there any chance, do you think?"

"No, I don't think there is," said Luke; for he was by no means anxious to have Harry in the same town.

"Then I shall probably stay with the professor."

"What do you do?"

"Take tickets at the door and help him beforehand with his apparatus."

"You'll let me in free, to-night, won't you?"

"That isn't for me to decide."

"I should think the professor would let your friends go in free."

"I'll make you an offer, Luke," said he.

"What is it?"

"Just pay me the rest of; that money to-night and I'll let you in free at my own expense."

"I can't do it. I haven't got the money. If 'you'll give it back, I'll call it a dollar more and pay you the whole at the end of next week."

"I'm afraid your calling it a dollar more wouldn't do much good," said Harry, shrewdly.

"Do you doubt my word?" blustered Luke, who had regained courage now that he had ascertained the real object of Harry's visit and that it had no connection with him.

"I won't express any opinion on that subject," answered Harry; "but there's an old saying that a 'bird in the hand's worth two in the bush.'"

"I hate old sayings."

"Some of them contain a great deal of truth."

"What a fool I was to pay him that five dollars!" thought Luke, regretfully. "If I hadn't been such a simpleton, I should have found out what brought him here, before throwing away nearly all I had."

This was the view Luke took of paying his debts. He regarded it as money thrown away. Apparently, a good many young men are of a similar opinion. This was not, however, according to Harry's code, and was never likely to be. He believed in honesty and integrity. If he hadn't, I should feel far less confidence in his ultimate success.

"I think I must leave you," said Harry, rising. "The professor may need me."

"Do you like him? Have you got a good place?"

"Yes, I like him. He is a very pleasant man."

"How does it pay?"

"Pretty well."

"I wouldn't mind trying it myself. Do you handle all the money?"

"I take the money at the door."

"I suppose you might keep back a dollar or so, every night, and he'd never know the difference."

"I don't know. I never thought about that," said Harry, dryly.

"Oh, I remember, you're one of the pious boys,"

"I'm too pious to take money that doesn't belong to me, if that's what you mean," said Harry.

This was a very innocent remark; but Luke, remembering how he had kept Harry's pocketbook, chose to interpret it as a fling to himself.

"Do you mean that for me?" he demanded, angrily.

"Mean what for you?"

"That about keeping other people's money."

"I wasn't talking about you at all. I was talking about myself."

"You'd better not insult me," said Luke, still suspicious.

"I'm not in the habit of insulting anybody."

"I don't believe in people that set themselves up to be so much better than everybody else."

"Do you mean that for me?" asked Harry, smiling.

"Yes, I do. What are you going to do about it?"

"Nothing, except to deny that I make any such claims. Shall you come round to the hall, to-night?"

"Perhaps so."

"Then I shall see you. I must be going now."

He went out, leaving Luke vainly deploring the loss of the five dollars which he had so foolishly squandered in paying his debt.

CHAPTER XXIX
IN THE PRINTING OFFICE

Harry," said the professor, after breakfast the next morning, "I find we must get some more bills printed. You may go round to the office of the Centreville Gazette, and ask them how soon they can print me a hundred large bills and a thousand small ones."

"All right, sir. Suppose they can't have them done by the ready to start?"

"They can send them to me by express."

Harry had never been in a printing office; but he had a great curiosity to see one ever since he had read the "Life of Benjamin Franklin." If there was anyone in whose steps he thought he should like to follow, it was Franklin, and Franklin was a printer.

He had no difficulty in finding the office. It was in the second story of a building, just at the junction of two roads near the center of the town, the post office being just underneath. He ascended a staircase, and saw on the door, at the head of the stairs:

"CENTREVILLE GAZETTE"

He opened the door and entered. He saw a large room, containing a press at the end, while two young men, with paper caps on their heads, were standing in their shirt sleeves at upright cases setting type. On one side there was a very small office partitioned off. Within, a man was seen seated at a desk, with a pile of exchange papers on the floor, writing busily. This was Mr. Jotham Anderson publisher and editor of the Gazette.

"I want to get some printing done," said Harry, looking toward the journeymen.

"Go to Mr. Anderson," said one, pointing to the office.

Harry went in. The editor looked up as he entered.

"What can I do for you?" he asked.

"I want to get some printing done."

"For yourself?"

"No; for Professor Henderson."

"I've done jobs for him before. What does he want?"

Our hero explained.

"Very well, we will do it."

"Can you have it done before two o'clock?"

"Impossible. I am just bringing out my paper."

"When can you have the job finished?"

"To-morrow noon."

"I suppose that will do. We perform to-morrow at Berlin and they can be sent over to the hotel there."

"You say 'we,'" answered Harry, amused. "I take tickets, and assist him generally."

"How do you like the business?"

"Very well; but I should like your business better."

"What makes you think so?"

"I have been reading the 'Life of Benjamin Franklin.' He was a printer."

"That's true; but I'm sorry to say Franklins are scarce in our printing offices. I never met one yet."

"I shouldn't expect to turn out a Franklins; but I think one couldn't help being improved by the business."

"True again, though, of course, it depends on the wish to improve. How long have you been working for Professor Henderson?"

"Not long. Only two or three weeks."

"What did you do before?"

"I was pegger in a shoe shop."

"Didn't you like it?"

"Well enough, for I needed to earn money and it paid me; but I don't think I should like to be a shoemaker all my life. It doesn't give any chance to learn."

"Then you like learning?"

"Yes. 'Live and learn'--that is my motto."

"It is a good one. Do you mean to be a printer?"

"If I get a chance."

"You may come into my office on the first of April, if you like. One of my men will leave me by the first of May. If you are a smart boy, and really wish to learn the business, you can break in so as to be useful in four weeks."

"I should like it," said Harry; "but," he added, with hesitation, "I am poor, and could not afford to work for nothing while I was learning."

"I'll tell you what I'll do, then," said the editor. "I'll give you your board for the first month, on condition that you'll work for six months afterwards for two dollars a week and board. That's a fair offer. I wouldn't make it if I didn't feel assured that you were smart, and would in time be valuable to me."

"I'll come if my father does not object."

"Quite tight. I should not like to have you act contrary to his wishes. I suppose, for the present, you will remain with Professor Henderson."

"Yes, sir."

"Very well. Let me hear from you when you have communicated with your father."

Harry left the office plunged in thought. It came upon him with surprise, that he had engaged himself to learn a new business, and that the one which he had longed to follow ever since he had become acquainted with Franklin's early life. He realized that he was probably making immediate sacrifice. He could, undoubtedly, make more money in the shoe shop than in the printing office, for the present at least. By the first of April the shoe business obtain employment. But then he was sure he should like printing better, and if he was ever going to change, why, the sooner he made the change the better.

When he returned to the hotel, he told the professor what he had done.

"I am glad you are not going at once," said his employer, "for I should be sorry to lose you. I generally give up traveling for the season about the first of April, so that I shall be ready to release you. I commend your choice of a trade. Many of our best editors have been practical printers in their youth."

"I should like to be an editor, but I don't know enough."

"Not at present; but you can qualify yourself to become one--that is, if you devote you spare time to reading and studying."

"I mean to do that."

"Then you will fair chance of becoming what you desire. To a certain extent, a boy, or young man, holds the future in his own hands."

Harry wrote to father, at once, in regard to the plan which he had in view. The answer did not reach him for nearly a week; but we will so far anticipate matters as to insert that part which related to it.

"If you desire to be a printer, Harry, I shall not object. It is a good trade, and you can make yourself, through it, useful to the community. I do not suppose it will ever make you rich. Still, I should think it might, in time, give you a comfortable living--better, I hope, than I have been able to earn as a farmer. If you determine to win success, you probably will. If you should leave your present place before the first of April, we shall be very glad to have you come home, if only for a day or two. We all miss you very much--your mother, particularly. Tom doesn't say much about it; but I know he will be as glad to see you as the rest of us."

Harry read this letter with great pleasure, partly because it brought him permission to do as he desired, and partly because it was gratifying to him to feel that he was missed at home. He determined, if it was a possible thing, to leave the professor a week before his new engagement, and spend that time in Granton.

CHAPTER XXX
THE YOUNG TREASURER

On the morning after receiving the letter from his father, Harry came down to breakfast, but looked in vain for the professor. Supposing he would be down directly, he sat down to the breakfast table. When he had nearly finished eating, a boy employed about the hotel came to his side.

"That gentleman you're with is sick. He wants you to come to his room as soon as you are through breakfast."

Harry did not wait to finish, but got up from the table at once, and went up to his employer's room.

"Are you sick, sir?" he inquired, anxiously.

The professor's face was flushed, and he was tossing about in bed.

"Yes," he answered. "I am afraid I am threatened with a fever."

"I hope not, sir."

"I am subject to fevers; but I hope I might not have another for some time to come. I must have caught cold yesterday, and the result is, that I am sick this morning."

"What can I do for you, sir?"

"I should like to have you go for the doctor. Inquire of the landlord who is the best in the village."

"I will go at once."

On inquiry, our hero was informed that Dr. Parker was the most trusted physician in the neighborhood, and he proceeded to his house at once. The doctor was, fortunately, still at home, and answered the summons immediately. He felt the sick man's pulse, asked him a variety of questions, and finally announced his opinion.

"You are about to have a fever," he said, "if, indeed, the fever has not already set in."

"A serious fever, doctor?" asked the sick man, anxiously.

"I cannot yet determine."

"Do you think I shall be long sick?"

"That, also, is uncertain. I suppose you will be likely to be detained here a fortnight, at least."

"I wish I could go home."

"It would not be safe for you to travel, under present circumstances."

"If I were at home, I could be under my wife's care."

"Can't she come here?"

"She has three young children. It would be difficult for her to leave them."

"Who is the boy that called at my house?"

"Harry Walton. He is my assistant--takes money at the door, and helps me other ways."

"Is he trustworthy?"

"I have always found him so."

"Why can't he, attend upon you?"

"I mean to retain him with me--that is, if he will stay. It will be dull work for a boy of his age."

"You can obtain a nurse, besides, if needful."

"You had better engage one for me, as I cannot confine him here all the time."

"I will do so. I know of one, skillful and experienced, who is just now at leisure. I will send her round here this morning."

"What is her name?"

"Not a very romantic one--Betsy Chase."

"I suppose that doesn't prevent her being a good nurse," said the professor, smiling.

"Not at all."

Here Harry entered the room.

"Harry," said the professor, "the doctor tells me I am going to be sick."

"I am very sorry, sir," said our hero, with an air of concern.

"I shall probably be detained here at least a fortnight. Are you willing to remain with me?"

"Certainly, sir. I should not think of leaving you, sick and alone, if you desired me to stay. I hope I can make myself useful to you."

"You can. I shall need you to do errands for me, and to sit with me a part of the time."

"I shall be very willing to do so, sir."

"You will probably find it dull."

"Not so dull as you will find it, sir. The time must seem very long to you, lying on that bed."

"I suppose it will; but that can't be helped."

"A nurse will be here this afternoon," said the doctor.

"Until she comes, you will be in attendance here."

"Yes, sir."

"I will direct you what to do, and how often to administer the medicines. Can remember?"

"Yes, sir, I shall not forget."

Dr. Parker here gave Harry minute instructions, which need not be repeated, since they were altogether of a professional nature.

After the doctor was gone, Professor Henderson said:

"As soon as the nurse comes, I shall want you to ride over to the next town, Carmansville, and countermand the notices for an exhibition to-night. I shall not be able to give entertainments for some time to come. Indeed, I am not sure but I must wait till next season."

"How shall I go over?" asked Harry.

"You may get a horse and buggy at the stable, and drive over there. If I remember rightly, it is between little seven and eight miles. The road is a little winding, but I think you won't lose your way."

"Oh, I'll find it," said Harry, confidently.

It was not till three o'clock that the nurse made her appearance, and it was past three before Harry started on his way.

"You need not hurry home," said the professor. "In fact, you had better take supper at the hotel in Carmansville, as you probably could not very well get back here till eight o'clock."

"Very well, sir," said Harry. "But shan't you need me?"

"No; Miss Chase will attend to me."

"Mrs. Chase, if you please," said the nurse. "I've been a widder for twenty years."

"I beg your pardon, Mrs. Chase," said the sick man smiling.

"When my husband was alive, I never expected to go out nursin'; but I've had come to it."

"The doctor says you are a very skillful and experienced nurse."

"I'd ought to be. I've nussed people in almost all sorts of diseases, from measles to smallpox. You needn't be frightened, sir; I haven't had any smallpox case lately. Isn't it most time to take your medicine?"

Harry left the room, and was soon on his way to Carmansville. Once he got off the road, which was rather a perplexing one, but he soon found it again. However, it was half past five before he reached the village, and nearly an hour later before he had done the errand which brought him over. Finally, he came back to the tavern, and being by this time hungry, went in at once to the tavern, and being by this time hungry, went in at once to supper. He did full justice to the meal which was set before him. The day was cold, and his ride had stimulated his appetite.

When he sat down to the table he was alone; but a minute afterward a small, dark-complexioned man, with heavy black whiskers, came in, and sat down beside him. He had a heavy look, and a forbidding expression; but our hero was too busy to take particular notice of him till the latter commenced a conversation.

"It's a pretty cold day," he remarked.

"Very cold," said Harry. "I am dreading my ride back to Pentland."

"Are you going to Pentland to-night?" asked the stranger, with interest.

"Yes, sir."

"Do you live over there?"

"No; I am there for a short time only," Harry replied.

"Business?"

"Yes."

"You seem rather young to be in business," said the stranger.

"Oh," said Harry, smiling, "I am in the employ of Professor Henderson, the ventriloquist. I suppose it is hardly proper to say that I am in business."

"Professor Henderson! Why, he is going to give an entertainment here to-night, isn't he?"

"He was; but I have come over to countermand the notice."

"What is that for?"

"He is taken sick at Pentland, and won't be able to come."

"Oh, that's it. Well, I'm sorry, for I should like to have gone to hear him. So you are his assistant, are you?"

"Yes, sir."

"Can you perform tricks, too?"

"I don't assist him in that way. I take money at the door, and help him with his apparatus."

"Have you been with him long?"

"Only a few weeks."

"So you are his treasurer, are you?" asked the stranger smiling.

"Ye--es," said Harry, slowly, for it brought to his mind that he had one hundred and fifty dollars of the professor's money in his pocket, besides the pocketbook containing his own. He intended to have left it with his employer, but in the hurry of leaving he had forgotten to do so. Now he was about to take a long ride in the evening with this large sum of money about him.

"However," he said, reassuring himself, "there is nothing to be afraid of. Country people are not robbers. Burglars stay in the cities. I have nothing to fear."

Still he prudently resolved, if compelled to be out late again, to leave his money at home.

He rose from table, followed by the stranger.

"Well," said the latter, "I must be going. How soon do you start?"

"In a few minutes."

"Well, good night."

"Good night."

"He seems inclined to be social," thought Harry, "but I don't fancy him much."

CHAPTER XXXI

H arry was soon on his way home. It was already getting dark, and he felt a little anxious lest he should lose his way. He was rather sorry that he had not started earlier, though he had lost no time.

He had gone about two miles, when he came to a place where two roads met. There was no guideboard, and he could not remember by which road he had come. Luckily, as he thought, he described a man a little ahead. He stopped the horse, and hailed him.

"Can you tell me which road to take to Pentland?" he asked.

The man addressed turned his head, and, to his surprise, our hero recognized his table companion at the inn.

"Oh, it's you, my young friend!" he said.

"Yes, sir. Can you tell me the right road to Pentland? I have never been this way before to-day, and I have forgotten how I came."

"I am thinking of going to Pentland myself," said the other.

"My sister lives there. If you don't mind giving me a lift, I will jump in with you, and guide you."

Now, though Harry did not fancy the man's appearance, he had no reason to doubt him, nor any ground for refusing his request.

"Jump in, sir," he said. "There is plenty of room."

The stranger was speedily seated at his side.

"Take the left-hand road," he said.

Harry turned to his left.

"It's rather a blind road," observed the stranger.

"I think I could remember in the daytime," said Harry; "but it is so dark now, that I am in doubt."

"So I suppose."

The road on which they had entered was very lonely. Scarcely a house was passed, and the neighborhood seemed quite uninhabited.

"I don't remember this road," said Harry, anxiously.

"Are you sure we are right?"

"Yes, yes, we are right. Don't trouble yourself."

"It's a lonely road."

"So it is. I don't suppose there's anybody lives within half a mile."

"The road didn't seem so lonely when I came over it this afternoon."

"Oh, that's the effect of sunshine. Nothing seems lonely in the daytime. Turn down that lane."

"What for?" asked Harry, in surprise. "That can't be the road to Pentland."

"Never mind that. Turn, I tell you."

His companion spoke fiercely, and Harry's mind began to conceive alarming suspicions as to his character. But he was brave, and not easily daunted.

"The horse and carriage are mine, or, at least, are under my direction," he said, firmly, "and you have no control over them. I shall not turn."

"Won't you?" retorted the stranger, with an oath, and drew from his pocket a pistol. "Won't you?"

"What do you mean? Who are you?" demanded Harry.

"You will find out before I get through with you. Now turn into the lane."

"I will not," said Harry, pale, but determined.

"Then I will save you the trouble," and his companion snatched the reins from him, and turned the horse himself. Resistance was, of course, useless, and our hero was compelled to submit.

"There, that suits me better. Now to business."

"To business. Produce your pocketbook."

"Would you rob me?" asked Harry, who was in a measure prepared for the demand.

"Oh, of course not," said the other. "Gentlemen never do such things. I want to burrow your money, that is all."

"I don't want to lend."

"I dare say not," sneered the other; "but I shan't be able to respect your wishes.

The sooner you give me the money the better."

Harry had two pocketbooks. The one contained his own money--about forty dollars--the other the money of his employer. The first was in the side pocket of his coat, the second in the pocket of his pants. The latter, as was stated in the preceding chapter, contained one hundred and fifty dollars. Harry heartily repented not having left it behind, but it was to late for repentance. He could only hope that the robber would be satisfied with one pocketbook, and not suspect the existence of the other. There seemed but little hope of saving his own money. However, he determined to do it, if possible.

"Hurry up," said the stranger, impatiently. "You needn't pretend you have no money. I know better than that. I saw you pay the landlord."

"Then he saw the professor's pocketbook," thought Harry, uneasily. "Mine is of different appearance. I hope he won't detect the difference."

"I hope you will leave me some of the money," said Harry, producing the pocketbook.

"It is all I have."

"How much is there?"

"About forty dollars."

"Humph! that isn't much."

"It is all I have in the world."

"Pooh! you are young and can soon earn some more. I must have the whole of it."

"Can't you leave me five dollars?"

"No, I can't. Forty dollars are little enough to serve my turn."

So saying, he coolly deposited the pocketbook in the pocket of his pants.

"So far so good. It's well, youngster, you didn't make any more fuss, or I might have had to use my little persuader"; and he displayed the pistol.

"Will you let me go now, sir?"

"I have not got through my business yet. That's a nice overcoat of yours."

Harry looked at him, in doubt as to his meaning, but he was soon enlightened.

"I am a small person," proceeded the man with black whiskers, "scarcely any larger than you. I think it'll be a good fit."

"Must I lose my overcoat, too?" thought Harry, in trouble.

"You've got an overcoat of your own, sir," he said.

"You don't need mine."

"Oh, I wouldn't rob you of yours on any account. A fair exchange is no robbery. I am going to give you mine in exchange for yours."

The stranger's coat was rough and well worn, and, at its best, had been inferior to Harry's coat. Our hero felt disturbed at the prospect of losing it, for he could not tell when he could afford to get another.

"I should think you might be satisfied with the pocketbook," he said. "I hope you will leave me my coat."

"Off with the coat, youngster!" was the sole reply.

"First, get out of the buggy. We can make the exchange better outside."

As opposition would be unavailing, Harry obeyed. The robber took from him the handsome overcoat, the possession of which had afforded him so much satisfaction, and handed him his own. In great disgust and dissatisfaction our hero invested himself in it.

"Fits you as if it was made for you," said the stranger, with a short laugh. "Yours is a trifle slow for me, but I can make it go. No, don't be in such a hurry."

He seized Harry by the arm as he was about to jump into the carriage.

"I must go," said Harry. "You have already detained me some time."

"I intend to detain you some time longer."

"Have you got any more business with me?"

"Yes, I have. You've hit it exactly. You'll soon know what it is."

He produced a ball of cord from a pocket of his inside coat, and with a knife severed a portion. "Do you know what this is for?" he asked, jeeringly.

"No."

"Say, 'No, sir.' It's more respectful. Well, I'll gratify your laudable curiosity. It's to tie your hands and feet."

"I won't submit to it," said Harry, angrily.

"Won't you?" asked the other, coolly. "This is a very pretty pistol, isn't it? I hope I shan't have to use it."

"What do you want to tie my hands for?" asked Harry.

"For obvious reasons, my young friend."

"I can't drive if my hands are tied."

"Correct, my son. I don't intend you to drive tonight. Give me your hands."

Harry considered whether it would be advisable to resist. The stranger was not much larger than himself. He was a man, however, and naturally stronger. Besides, he had a pistol. He seceded that it was necessary to submit. After all, he had saved his employer's money, even if he had lost his own, and this was something. He allowed himself to be bound.

"Now," said the stranger, setting him up against the stone wall, which bordered the lane, "I will bid you good night. I might take your horse, but, on the whole, I don't want him. I will fasten him to this tree, where he will be all ready for you in the morning. That's considerate in me. Good night. I hope you are comfortable."

He disappeared in the darkness, and Harry was left alone.

CHAPTER XXXII
THE GOOD SAMARITAN

Harry's reflections, as he sat on the ground were not the most cheerful. He was sitting in a constrained posture, his hands and feet being tied, and, moreover, the cold air chilled him. The cold was not intense, but as he was unable to move his limbs he, of course, felt it the more.

"I suppose it will get colder," thought Harry, uncomfortably. "I wonder if there is any danger of freezing."

The horse evidently began to feel impatient, for he turned round and looked at our hero. "Why don't you keep on?"

"I wish somebody would come this way," thought Harry, and he looked up and down the lane as well as he could, but could see no one.

"If I could only get at my knife," said Harry, to himself, "I could cut theses cords. Let me try."

He tried to get his hands into his pockets, but it was of no avail. The pocket was too deep, and though he worked his body round, he finally gave it up. It seemed likely that he must stay here all night. The next day probably some one would come by, as they were so near a public road, upon whom he could call to release him.

"The night will seem about a week long," poor Harry considered. "I shan't dare to go to sleep, for fear I may freeze to death."

The horse whinnied again, and again looked inquiringly at his young driver, but the latter was not master of the situation, and was obliged to disregard the mute appeal.

"I wonder the robber didn't carry off the horse," thought Harry. "I suppose he had his reasons. It isn't likely he left him out of his regard for me."

Two hours passed, and Harry still found himself a prisoner. His constrained position became still more uncomfortable. He longed for the power of jumping up and stretching his legs, now numb and chilled, but the cord was strong, and defied his efforts. No person had passed, not had he heard any sound as he lay there, except the occasional whinny of the horse which was tied as well as himself, and did not appear to enjoy his confinement any better.

It was at this moment that Harry's heart leaped with sudden hope, as he heard in the distance the sound of a whistle. It might be a boy, or it might be a man; but, as he listened intently, he perceived that it was coming nearer.

"I hope I can make him hear," thought Harry, earnestly.

It was a boy of about his own age, who was advancing along the road from which he had turned into the lane. The boy was not alone, as it appeared, for a large dog ran before him. The dog first noticed the horse and buggy, and next our hero, lying on the ground, and, concluding that something was wrong, began to bark violently, circling uncomfortably near Harry, against whom he seemed to cherish hostile designs.

"What's the matter, Caesar?" shouted his young master.

"Good dog!" said Harry, soothingly, in momentary fear that the brute would bite him.

But Caesar was not to be cajoled by flattery. "Bow, wow, wow!" he answered, opening his large mouth, and displaying a formidable set of teeth.

"Good dog! I'd like to choke him!" added Harry, in an undertone to himself.

There was another volley of barks, which seemed likely to be followed by an attack. Just at this moment, however, luckily for our hero, the dog's master came up.

"Why, Caesar," he called, "what is the matter with you?"

"Please take your dog away," said Harry. "I am afraid he will bite me."

"Who are you?" inquired the boy, in surprise.

"Come and untie these cords, and I will tell you."

"What! Are you tied?"

"Yes, hand and foot."

"Who did it?" asked the boy, in increasing surprise.

"I don't know his name, but he robbed me of my pocketbook before doing it."

"What, a robber around here!" exclaimed the boy, incredulous.

"Yes; I met him first over in Carmansville. Thank you; now my feet if you please. It seems good to be free again"; and Harry swung his arms, and jumped up and down to bring back the sense of warmth to his chilled limbs.

"Is this horse yours?" asked the boy.

"Yes; I took up the man and he promised to show me the road to Pentland."

"This isn't the road to Pentland."

"I suppose not. He took me wrong on purpose."

"How much money did he take from you?"

"Forty dollars."

"That's a good deal," said the country boy. "Was it yours?"

"Yes."

"I never had so much money in my life."

"It has taken me almost six months to earn it. But I had more money with me, only he didn't know it."

"How much?"

"A hundred and fifty dollars."

"Was it yours?" asked the boy, surprised.

"No; it belonged to my employer."

"Who is he?"

"Professor Henderson, the ventriloquist."

"Where is he stopping?"

"Over at Pentland. He is sick at the hotel there."

"It's lucky for you I was out to-night. I ain't often out so late but I went to see a friend of mine, and stayed later than I meant to."

"Do you live near here?"

"I live about a quarter of a mile up this lane."

"Do you know what time it is?"

"I don't know, but I think it is past ten."

"I wonder whether I can get anybody to go with me to Pentland. I can't find my way in the dark."

"I will go with you to-morrow morning."

"But what shall I do to-night?"

"I'll tell you. Come home with me. The folks will take you in, and the horse can be put up in the barn."

Harry hesitated

"I suppose they will feel anxious about me over at Pentland. They won't know what has become of me."

"You can start early in the morning--as early as you like."

"Perhaps it will be better," said Harry, after a pause.

"It won't trouble your family too much, will it?"

"Not a bit," answered the boy, heartily. "Very likely they won't know till morning," he added, laughing. "They go to bed early, and I told them they needn't wait up for me."

"I am very much obliged to you," said Harry. "I will accept your kind invitation. As I've got a horse, we may as well ride. I'll untie him, and you jump into the buggy."

"All right," said the boy, well pleased.

"You may drive, for you know the way better than I."

"Where did this horse come from?"

"From the stable in Pentland."

"Perhaps they will think you have run away with it."

"I hope not."

"What is your name?"

"Harry Walton. What is yours?"

"Jefferson Selden. The boys usually call me Jeff."

"Is that your dog?"

"Yes. He's a fine fellow."

"I didn't think so when he was threatening to bite me," said Harry laughing.

"I used to be afraid of dogs," said Jeff; "but I got cured of it after a while. When I go out at night, I generally take Caesar with me. If you had had him, you would have been a match for the robber."

"He had a pistol."

"Caesar would have had him down before he could use it."

"I wish he had been with me, then."

They had, by this time, come in sight of Jeff's house. It was a square farmhouse, with a barn in the rear.

"We'll go right out to the barn," said Jeff, "and put up the horse. Then we'll come back to the house and go to bed."

There was a little difficulty in unharnessing the horse, on account of the absence of light; but at last, by a combined effort, it was done, and the buggy was drawn into the barn and the doors shut.

"There, all will be safe till to-morrow morning," said Jeff. "Now we'll go into the house."

He entered by the back shed door, and Harry followed him. They went into the broad, low kitchen, with its ample fireplace, in which a few embers were glowing. By these Jeff lighted a candle, and asked Harry if he would have anything to eat.

"No, thank you," said Harry. "I ate a hearty supper at Carmansville."

"Then we'll go upstairs to bed. I sleep in a small room over the shed. You won't mind sleeping with me?"

"I should like your company," said Harry, who was attracted to his good-natured companion.

"Then come up. I guess we'll find the bed wide enough."

He led the way up a narrow staircase, into a room low studded, and very plainly but comfortably furnished.

"The folks will be surprised to see you here in the morning," said Jeff.

"I may be gone before they are up."

"I guess not. Father'll be up by five o'clock, and I think that'll be as early as you'll want to be stirring."

CHAPTER XXXIII
THE REWARD OF FIDELITY

"Where am I?" asked Harry, the next morning, as he sat up in bed and stared around him.

"Don't you remember?" asked Jeff, smiling.

Jeff was standing by the bedside, already dressed.

"Yes; I remember now," said Harry, slowly. "What time is it?"

"Seven o'clock."

"Seven o'clock! I meant to be dressed at six."

"That is the time I got up," said Jeff.

"Why didn't you wake me up?"

"You looked so comfortable that I thought it was a pity to wake you. You must have felt tired."

"I think it was the cold that made me sleepy. I got chilled through when I lay on the ground there, tied hand and foot. But I must get up in hurry now."

He jumped out of bed, and hurried on his clothes.

"Now," said Jeff, "come down into the kitchen, and mother'll give you some breakfast."

"I am giving you a great deal of trouble, I am afraid," said Harry.

"No, you're not. It's no trouble at all. The rest of the family have eaten breakfast, but I waited for you. I've been up an hour, and feel as hungry as a wolf. So come down, and we'll see who'll eat the most."

"I can do my part," said Harry. "I've got a good appetite, though I've been up a food deal less than an hour."

"Take your overcoat alone," said Jeff; "or will you come up and get after breakfast?"

"I'll take it down with me. It isn't my coat, you know. Mine was a much better one. I wish I had it back."

Jeff, meanwhile, had taken up the coat.

"There's something in the pocket," he said. "What is it?"

"I didn't put anything in."

Harry thrust his hand into the side pocket for the first time, and drew out a shabby leather wallet.

"Perhaps there's money in it," Jeff suggested.

The same thought had occurred to Harry. He hastily opened it, and his eyes opened wide with astonishment as he drew out a thick roll of bills.

"By hokey!" said Jeff, "you're in luck. The robber took your pocketbook, and left his own. Maybe there's as much as you lost. Count it."

This Harry eagerly proceeded to do.

"Three--eight--eleven--thirteen--twenty," he repeated, aloud. He continued his count, which resulted in showing that the wallet contained ninety-seven dollars.

"Ninety-seven dollars!" exclaimed Jeff. "How much did you lose?"

"Forty dollars."

"Then you've made just fifty-seven dollars. Bully for you!"

"But I've exchanged a good overcoat for a poor one."

"There can't be more than seventeen dollars difference."

"Not so much."

"Then you're forty dollars better off, at any rate."

"But I don't know as I can claim this money," said Harry, doubtfully. "It isn't mine."

"He won't be likely to call for it. When he does, and returns you the money and the coat, it will be time to think about it."

"I will ask Professor Henderson about that. At any rate I've got my money back, that's one good thing."

This timely discovery made Harry decidedly cheerful, and, if anything, sharpened his appetite for breakfast.

Now Mr. Selden had gone out to oversee some farm work; but Mrs. Selden received out hero very kindly, and made him feel that he was heartily welcome to that she could offer. She had many questions to ask about the bold robber who had waylaid him, and expressed the hope that he had left the neighborhood.

"Perhaps he'll come back for his wallet, Harry," said Jeff. "You'd better look out for him."

"I shall take care how I carry much money about with me, after this," said Harry. "That was what got me into a scrape yesterday."

"He wouldn't make out much if he tried to rob me," said Jeff. "I haven't got money enough about me to pay the board of a full-grown fly for twenty-four hours."

"You don't look as if your poverty troubled you much," said his mother.

"I don't have any board bills to pay," said Jeff, "so I can get along."

"I should think you would feel nervous about riding to Pentland alone," said Mrs. Selden, "for fear of meeting the man who robbed you yesterday."

"I do dread it a little," said Harry, "having so much money about me. Besides this ninety-seven dollars, I've got a hundred and fifty dollars belonging to my employer."

"Suppose I go with you to protect you," said Jeff.

"I wish you would."

"I don't think Jefferson would make a very efficient protector," said his mother.

"You don't know how brave I am, mother," said Jeff, in the tone of an injured hero.

"No, I don't," said his mother, smiling. "I believe there was a time when you were not very heroic in the company of dogs."

"That's long ago, mother. I've got over it now."

"If you would like to ride over with your friend, you may do so. But how will you get back?"

"Major Pinkham will be up there this afternoon. I can wait, and ride home with him."

"Very well; I have no objection."

The two boys rode off together. Harry was glad to have a companion who knew the road well, for he did not care to be lost again till he had delivered up the money which he had in charge. There was no opportunity to test Jeff's courage, for the highwayman did not make his appearance. Indeed, it was not till the next morning that he discovered the serious blunder he had made in leaving his own wallet behind, and, though he was angry and disgusted, prudential considerations prevented his going back. He was forced to the unpleasant conviction that he had overreached himself, and that his intended victim had come out best in the "exchange" which "was no robbery." I may as well add here that, though he deserved to be caught, he was not, and Harry has never, to this day, set eyes either upon him or upon the coat.

When Harry arrived at Pentland, he found that no little anxiety had been felt about him.

"Has Harry come yet?" asked the sick man, at ten o'clock the evening previous.

"No, he hasn't," answered the nurse.

"It's strange what keeps him."

"Did he have any money of yours with him?"

"Yes, I believe he had."

"Oh!" ejaculated Mrs. Chase, significantly.

"What do you mean by that?"

"I didn't say anything, did I?"

"I am afraid he may have been attacked and robbed on the road."

Mrs. Chase coughed.

"Don't you think so?"

"I'll tell you what I think, professor," said the nurse, proceeding to speak plainly, "I don't think you'll ever see anything of that boy ag'in."

"Why not?"

"It ain't safe to trust boys with money," she answered, sententiously.

"Oh, I'm not afraid of his honesty."

"You don't say! Maybe you haven't seen as much of boys as I have."

"I was once a boy myself," said the professor, smiling.

"Oh, you--that's different."

"Why is it different? I wasn't any better than boys generally."

"I don't know anything about that; but you mark my words--as like as not he's run away with your money. How much did he have?"

"I can't say exactly. Over a hundred dollars, I believe."

"Then he won't come back," said Mrs. Chase, decidedly.

Here the conference closed, as it was necessary for Mr. Henderson to take medicine.

"Has the boy returned?" asked the professor, the next morning.

"You don't expect him--do you?"

"Certainly I expect him."

"Well, he ain't come, and I guess he won't come."

"I am sure that boy is honest," said Professor Henderson to himself. "If he isn't, I'll never trust a boy again."

Mrs. Chase was going downstairs with her patient's breakfast dishes, when she was nearly run into by our hero, who had just returned, and was eager to report to his employer.

"Do be keerful," she expostulated, when, to her surprise, she recognized Harry.

So he had come back, after all, and falsified her prediction. Such is human nature, that for an instant she was disappointed.

"Here's pretty work," she said, "stayin' out all night, and worryin' the professor out of his wits."

"I couldn't help it, Mrs. Chase."

"Why couldn't you help it, I'd like to know?"

"I'll tell you afterwards. I must go up now, and see the professor."

Mrs. Chase was so curious that she returned, with the dishes, to hear Harry's statement.

"Good morning," said Harry, entering the chamber.

"I'm sorry to have been so long away, but I couldn't help it. I hope you haven't worried much about my absence."

"I knew you would come back, but Mrs. Chase had her doubts," said Professor Henderson, pleasantly. "Now tell me what it was that detained you?"

"A highwayman," said Harry.

"A highwayman!" exclaimed both in concert.

"Yes, I'll tell you all about it. But first, I'll say that he stole only my money, and didn't suspect that I had a hundred and fifty dollars of yours with me. That's all safe. Here it is. I think you had better take care of that yourself, sir, hereafter."

The professor glanced significantly at Mr. Chase, as much as to say, "You see how unjust your suspicions were. I am right, after all."

"Tell us all about it, Harry."

Our hero obeyed instructions; but it is not necessary to repeat a familiar tale.

"Massy sakes!" ejaculated Betsy Chase. "Who ever heerd the like?"

"I congratulate you, Harry, on coming off with such flying colors. I will, at my own expense, provide you with a new overcoat, as a reward for bringing home my money safe. You shall not lose anything by your fidelity."

CHAPTER XXXIV
IN DIFFICULTY

We must now transfer the scene to the Walton homestead. It looks very much the same as on the day when the reader was first introduced to it. There is not a single article of new furniture, nor is any of the family any better dressed. Poverty reigns with undisputed sway. Mr. Walton is reading a borrowed newspaper by the light of a candle--for it is evening--while Mrs. Walton is engaged in her never-ending task of mending old clothes, in the vain endeavor to make them look as well as new. It is so seldom that anyone of the family has new clothes, that the occasion is one long remembered and dated from.

"It seems strange we don't hear from Harry," said Mrs. Walton, looking up from her work.

"When was the last letter received?" asked Mr. Walton, laying down the paper.

"Over a week ago. He wrote that the professor was sick, and he was stopping at the hotel to take care of him."

"I remember. What was the name of the place?"

"Pentland."

"Perhaps his employer is recovered, and he is going about with him."

"Perhaps so; but I should think he would write. I am afraid he is sick himself. He may have caught the same fever."

"It is possible; but I think Harry would let us know in some way. At any rate, it isn't best to worry ourselves about uncertainties."

"I wonder if Harry's grown?" said Tom.

"Of course he's grown," said Mary.

"I wonder if he's grown as much as I have," said Tom, complacently.

"I don't believe you've grown a bit."

"Yes, I have; if you don't believe it, see how short my pants are."

Tom did, indeed, seem to be growing out of his pants, which were undeniably too short for him.

"You ought to have some new pants," said his mother, sighing; "but I don't see where the money is to come from."

"Nor I," said Mr. Walton, soberly. "Somehow I don't seem to get ahead at all. To-morrow my note for the cow comes due, and I haven't but two dollars to meet it."

"How large it the note?"

"With six months' interest, it amounts to forty-one dollars and twenty cents."

"The cow isn't worth that. She doesn't give as much milk as the one we lost."

"That's true. It was a hard bargain, but I could do no better."

"You say you won't be able to meet the payment. What will be the consequence?"

"I suppose Squire Green will take back the cow."

"Perhaps you can get another somewhere else, on better terms."

"I am afraid my credit won't be very good. I agreed to forfeit ten dollars to Squire Green, if I couldn't pay at the end of six months."

"Will he insist on that condition?"

"I am afraid he will. He is a hard man."

"Then," said Mrs. Walton, indignantly, "he won't deserve to prosper."

"Worldly prosperity doesn't always go by merit. Plenty of mean men prosper."

Before Mrs. Walton had time to reply, a knock was heard at the door.

"Go to the door, Tom," said his father.

Tom obeyed, and shortly reappeared, followed by a small man with a thin figure and wrinkled face, whose deep-set, crafty eyes peered about him curiously as he entered the room.

"Good evening, Squire Green," said Mr. Walton, politely, guessing his errand.

"Good evenin', Mrs. Walton. The air's kinder frosty. I ain't so young as I was once, and it chills my blood."

"Come up to the fire, Squire Green," said Mrs. Walton, who wanted the old man to be comfortable, though she neither liked nor respected him.

The old man sat down and spread his hands before the fire.

"Anything new stirring, Squire?" asked Hiram Walton.

"Nothin' that I know on. I was lookin' over my papers to-night, neighbor, and I come across that note you give for the cow. Forty dollars with interest, which makes the whole come to forty-one dollars and twenty cents. To-morrow's the day for payin'. I suppose you'll be ready?" and the old man peered at Hiram Walton with his little keen eyes.

"Now for it," thought Hiram. "I'm sorry to say, Squire Green," he answered, "that I can't pay the note. Times have been hard, and my family expenses have taken all I could earn."

The squire was not much disappointed, for now he was entitled to exact the forfeit of ten dollars.

"The contrack provides that if you can't meet the note you shall pay ten dollars," he said. "I 'spose you can do that."

"Squire Green, I haven't got but two dollars laid by."

"Two dollars!" repeated the squire, frowning. "That ain't honest. You knew the note was comin' due, and you'd oughter have provided ten dollars, at least."

"I've done as much as I could. I've wanted to meet the note, but I couldn't make money, and I earned all I could."

"You hain't been equinomical," said the squire, testily. "Folks can't expect to lay up money ef they spend it fast as it comes in"; and he thumped on the floor with his cane.

"I should like to have you tell us how we can economize any more than we have," said Mrs. Walton, with spirit. "Just look around you, and see if you think we have been extravagant in buying clothes. I am sure I have to darn and mend till I am actually ashamed."

"There's other ways of wastin' money," said the squire. "If you think we live extravagantly, come in any day to dinner, and we will convince you to the contrary," said Mrs. Walton, warmly.

"Tain't none of my business, as long as you pay me what you owe me," said the squire. "All I want is my money, and I'd orter have it."

"It doesn't seem right that my husband should forfeit ten dollars and lose the cow."

"That was the contrack, Mrs. Walton. Your husband 'greed to it, and--"

"That doesn't make it just."

"Tain't no more'n a fair price for the use of the cow six months. Ef you'll pay the ten dollars to-morrow, I'll let you have the cow six months longer on the same contrack."

"I don't see any possibility of my paying you the money, Squire Green. I haven't got it."

"Why don't you borrer somewhere?"

"I might as well owe you as another man, Besides, I don't know anybody that would lend me the money."

"You haven't tried, have you?"

"No."

"Then you'd better. I thought I might as well come round and remind you of the note as you might forget it."

"Not much danger," said Hiram Walton. "I've had it on my mind ever since I gave it."

"Well, I'll come round to-morrow night, and I hope you'll be ready. Good night."

No very cordial good night followed Squire Green as he hobbled out of the cottage--for he was lame--not--I am sure the reader will agree with me--did he deserve any. He was a mean, miserly, grasping man, who had no regard for the feelings or comfort of anyone else; whose master passion was a selfish love of accumulating money. His money did him little good, however, for he was as mean with himself as with others, and grudged himself even the necessaries of life, because, if purchased, it must be at the expense of his hoards. The time would come when he and his money must part, but he did not think of that.

CHAPTER XXXV
SETTLED

There was a general silence after Squire Green's departure. Hiram Walton looked gloomy, and the rest of the family also.

"What an awful mean man the squire is!" Tom broke out, indignantly.

"You're right, for once," said Mary.

In general, such remarks were rebuked by the father or mother; but the truth of Tom's observation was so clear, that for once he was not reproved.

"Squire Green's money does him very little good," said Hiram Walton. "He spends very little of it on himself, and it certainly doesn't obtain him respect in the village. Rich as he is, and poor as I am, I would rather stand in my shoes than his."

"I should think so," said his wife. "Money isn't everything."

"No; but it is a good deal I have suffered too much from the want of it, to despise it."

"Well, Hiram," said Mrs. Walton, who felt that it would not do to look too persistently upon the dark side, "you know that the song says, 'There's a good time coming.'"

"I've waited for it a long time, wife," said the farmer, soberly.

"Wait a little longer," said Mrs. Walton, quoting the refrain of the song.

He smiled faintly.

"Very well, I'll wait a little longer; but if I have to wait too long, I shall get discouraged."

"Children, it's time to go to bed," said Mrs. Walton.

"Mayn't I sit up a little longer?" pleaded Mary.

"'Wait a little longer,' mother," said Tom, laughing, as he quoted his mother's words against her.

"Ten minutes, only, then."

Before the ten minutes were over, there was great and unexpected joy in the little house. Suddenly the outer door opened, and, without the slightest warning to anyone, Harry walked in. He was immediately surrounded by the delighted family, and in less time than I am taking to describe it he had shaken hands with his father, kissed his mother and sister, and given Tom a bearlike hug, which nearly suffocated him.

"Where did you come from, Harry?" asked Mary.

"Dropped down from the sky," said Harry, laughing.

"Has the professor been giving exhibitions up there?" asked Tom.

"I've discharge the professor," said Harry, gayly. "I'm my own man now."

"And you've come home to stay, I hope," said his mother.

"Not long, mother," said Harry. "I can only stay a few days."

"What a bully overcoat you've got on!" said Tom.

"The professor gave it to me."

"Hasn't he got one for me, too?"

Harry took off his overcoat, and Tom was struck with fresh admiration as he surveyed his brother's inside suit.

"I guess you spent all you money on clothes," he said.

"I hope not," said Mr. Walton, whom experience had made prudent.

"Not quite all," said Harry, cheerfully. "How much money do you think I have brought home?"

"Ten dollars," said Tom.

"More."

"Fifteen."

"More."

"Twenty," said Mary.

"More."

"Twenty-five."

"I won't keep you guessing all night. What do you say to fifty dollars?"

"Oh, what a lot of money!" said Mary.

"You have done well, my son," said Mr. Walton. "You must have been very economical."

"I tried to be, father. But I didn't say fifty dollars was all I had."

"You haven't got more?" said his mother, incredulously.

"I've got a hundred dollars, mother," said Harry.

"Here are fifty dollars for you, father. It'll pay your note to Squire Green, and a little over. Here are thirty dollars, mother, of which you must use for ten for yourself, ten for Mary, and ten for Tom. I want you all to have some new clothes, to remember me by."

"But Harry, you will have nothing left for yourself."

"Yes, I shall. I have kept twenty dollars, which will be enough till I can earn some more."

"I don't see how you could save so much money, Harry," said his father.

"It was partly luck, father, and partly hard work. I'll tell you all about it."

He sat down before the fire and they listened to his narrative.

"Well, Harry," said Mr. Walton, "I am very glad to find that you are more fortunate than your father. I have had a hard struggle; but I will not complain if my children can prosper."

The cloud that Squire Green had brought with him had vanished, and all was sunshine and happiness.

It was agreed that no hint should be given to Squire Green that his note was to be paid. He did not even hear of Harry's arrival, and was quite unconscious of any change in the circumstances of the family, when he entered the cottage the next evening.

"Well, neighbor," he said, "I've brought along that ere note. I hope you've raised the money to pay it."

"Where do you think I could raise money, Squire?" asked Hiram Walton.

"I thought mebbe some of the neighbors would lent it to you."

"Money isn't very plenty with any of them, Squire, except with you."

"I calc'late better than they. Hev you got the ten dollars that you agreed to pay ef you couldn't meet the note?"

"Yes," said Hiram, "I raised the ten dollars."

"All right," said the squire, briskly, "I thought you could. As long as you pay that, you can keep the cow six months more, one a new contrack."

"Don't you think, Squire, it's rather hard on a poor man, to make him forfeit ten dollars because he can't meet his note?"

"A contrack's a contrack," said the squire. "It's the only way to do business."

"I think you are taking advantage of me, Squire."

"No, I ain't. You needn't hev come to me ef you didn't want to. I didn't ask you to buy the cow. I'll trouble you for that ten dollars, neighbor, as I'm in a hurry."

"On the whole, Squire, I think I'll settle up the note. That'll be cheaper than paying the forfeit."

"What! Pay forty-one dollars and twenty cents!" ejaculated the squire, incredulously.

"Yes; it's more than the cow's worth, but as I agreed to pay it I suppose I must."

"I thought you didn't hev the money," said the squire, his lower jaw falling; for he would have preferred the ten dollars' forfeit, and a renewal of the usurious contract.

"I didn't have it when you were in last night; but I've raised it since."

"You said you couldn't borrow it."

"I didn't borrow it."

"Then where did it come from?"

"My son Harry has got home, Squire. He has supplied me with the money."

"You don't say! Where is he? Been a-doin' well, has he?"

"Harry!"

Harry entered the room, and nodded rather coldly to the squire, who was disposed to patronize him, now that he was well dressed, and appeared to be doing well.

"I'm glad to see ye, Harry. So you've made money, have ye?"

"A little."

"Hev you come home to stay?"

"No sir; I shall only stay a few days."

"What hev ye been doin'"

"I am going to be a printer."

"You don't say! Is it a good business?"

"I think it will be," said Harry. "I can tell better by and by."

"Well, I'm glad you're doin' so well, Neighbor Walton, when you want another cow I'll do as well by you as anybody. I'll give you credit for another on the same terms."

"If I conclude to buy any, Squire, I may come round."

"Well, good night, all. Harry, you must come round and see me before you go back."

Harry thanked him, but did not propose to accept the invitation. He felt that the squire was no true friend, either to himself or to his family, and he should feel no pleasure in his society. It was not in his nature to be hypocritical, and he expressed no pleasure at the squire's affability and politeness.

I have thus detailed a few of Harry's early experiences; but I am quite aware that I have hardly fulfilled the promise of the title. He has neither lived long nor learned much as yet, nor has he risen very high in the world. In fact, he is still at the bottom of the ladder. I propose, therefore, to devote another volume to his later fortunes, and hope, in the end, to satisfy the reader. The most that can be said thus far is, that he has made a fair beginning, and I must refer the reader who is interested to know what success he met with as a printer, to the next volume, which will be entitled:

RISEN FROM THE RANKS;
OR
Harry Walton's Success.

The Codes Of Hammurabi And Moses
W. W. Davies

QTY

The discovery of the Hammurabi Code is one of the greatest achievements of archaeology, and is of paramount interest, not only to the student of the Bible, but also to all those interested in ancient history...

Religion   **ISBN:** *1-59462-338-4*   **Pages:132**

MSRP $12.95

The Theory of Moral Sentiments
Adam Smith

QTY

This work from 1749. contains original theories of conscience amd moral judgment and it is the foundation for systemof morals.

Philosophy   ISBN: *1-59462-777-0*   **Pages:536**

MSRP $19.95

Jessica's First Prayer
Hesba Stretton

QTY

In a screened and secluded corner of one of the many railway-bridges which span the streets of London there could be seen a few years ago, from five o'clock every morning until half past eight, a tidily set-out coffee-stall, consisting of a trestle and board, upon which stood two large tin cans, with a small fire of charcoal burning under each so as to keep the coffee boiling during the early hours of the morning when the work-people were thronging into the city on their way to their daily toil...

Pages:84

Childrens   ISBN: *1-59462-373-2*   *MSRP $9.95*

My Life and Work
Henry Ford

QTY

Henry Ford revolutionized the world with his implementation of mass production for the Model T automobile. Gain valuable business insight into his life and work with his own auto-biography... "We have only started on our development of our country we have not as yet, with all our talk of wonderful progress, done more than scratch the surface. The progress has been wonderful enough but..."

Pages:300

Biographies/   **ISBN:** *1-59462-198-5*   *MSRP $21.95*

The Art of Cross-Examination
Francis Wellman

QTY

I presume it is the experience of every author, after his first book is published upon an important subject, to be almost overwhelmed with a wealth of ideas and illustrations which could readily have been included in his book, and which to his own mind, at least, seem to make a second edition inevitable. Such certainly was the case with me; and when the first edition had reached its sixth impression in five months, I rejoiced to learn that it seemed to my publishers that the book had met with a sufficiently favorable reception to justify a second and considerably enlarged edition. ..

Reference   ISBN: *1-59462-647-2*

Pages:412
MSRP *$19.95*

On the Duty of Civil Disobedience
Henry David Thoreau

QTY

Thoreau wrote his famous essay, On the Duty of Civil Disobedience, as a protest against an unjust but popular war and the immoral but popular institution of slave-owning. He did more than write—he declined to pay his taxes, and was hauled off to gaol in consequence. Who can say how much this refusal of his hastened the end of the war and of slavery ?

Law   ISBN: *1-59462-747-9*

Pages:48
MSRP *$7.45*

Dream Psychology Psychoanalysis for Beginners
Sigmund Freud

QTY

Sigmund Freud, born Sigismund Schlomo Freud (May 6, 1856 - September 23, 1939), was a Jewish-Austrian neurologist and psychiatrist who co-founded the psychoanalytic school of psychology. Freud is best known for his theories of the unconscious mind, especially involving the mechanism of repression; his redefinition of sexual desire as mobile and directed towards a wide variety of objects; and his therapeutic techniques, especially his understanding of transference in the therapeutic relationship and the presumed value of dreams as sources of insight into unconscious desires.

Psychology   ISBN: *1-59462-905-6*

Pages:196
MSRP *$15.45*

The Miracle of Right Thought
Orison Swett Marden

QTY

Believe with all of your heart that you will do what you were made to do. When the mind has once formed the habit of holding cheerful, happy, prosperous pictures, it will not be easy to form the opposite habit. It does not matter how improbable or how far away this realization may see, or how dark the prospects may be, if we visualize them as best we can, as vividly as possible, hold tenaciously to them and vigorously struggle to attain them, they will gradually become actualized, realized in the life. But a desire, a longing without endeavor, a yearning abandoned or held indifferently will vanish without realization.

Self Help   ISBN: *1-59462-644-8*

Pages:360
MSRP *$25.45*

The Rosicrucian Cosmo-Conception Mystic Christianity *by Max Heindel* ISBN: *1-59462-188-8* **$38.95**
The Rosicrucian Cosmo-conception is not dogmatic, neither does it appeal to any other authority than the reason of the student. It is: not controversial, but is: sent forth in the, hope that it may help to clear... New Age/Religion Pages 646

Abandonment To Divine Providence *by Jean-Pierre de Caussade* ISBN: *1-59462-228-0* **$25.95**
"The Rev. Jean Pierre de Caussade was one of the most remarkable spiritual writers of the Society of Jesus in France in the 18th Century. His death took place at Toulouse in 1751. His works have gone through many editions and have been republished... Inspirational/Religion Pages 400

Mental Chemistry *by Charles Haanel* ISBN: *1-59462-192-6* **$23.95**
Mental Chemistry allows the change of material conditions by combining and appropriately utilizing the power of the mind. Much like applied chemistry creates something new and unique out of careful combinations of chemicals the mastery of mental chemistry... New Age Pages 354

The Letters of Robert Browning and Elizabeth Barret Barrett 1845-1846 vol II ISBN: *1-59462-193-4* **$35.95**
by Robert Browning and Elizabeth Barrett Biographies Pages 596

Gleanings In Genesis (volume I) *by Arthur W. Pink* ISBN: *1-59462-130-6* **$27.45**
Appropriately has Genesis been termed "the seed plot of the Bible" for in it we have, in germ form, almost all of the great doctrines which are afterwards fully developed in the books of Scripture which follow... Religion/Inspirational Pages 420

The Master Key *by L. W. de Laurence* ISBN: *1-59462-001-6* **$30.95**
In no branch of human knowledge has there been a more lively increase of the spirit of research during the past few years than in the study of Psychology, Concentration and Mental Discipline. The requests for authentic lessons in Thought Control, Mental Discipline and... New Age/Business Pages 422

The Lesser Key Of Solomon Goetia *by L. W. de Laurence* ISBN: *1-59462-092-X* **$9.95**
This translation of the first book of the "Lernegton" which is now for the first time made accessible to students of Talismanic Magic was done, after careful collation and edition, from numerous Ancient Manuscripts in Hebrew, Latin, and French... New Age/Occult Pages 92

Rubaiyat Of Omar Khayyam *by Edward Fitzgerald* ISBN:*1-59462-332-5* **$13.95**
Edward Fitzgerald, whom the world has already learned, in spite of his own efforts to remain within the shadow of anonymity, to look upon as one of the rarest poets of the century, was born at Bredfield, in Suffolk, on the 31st of March, 1809. He was the third son of John Purcell... Music Pages 172

Ancient Law *by Henry Maine* ISBN: *1-59462-128-4* **$29.95**
The chief object of the following pages is to indicate some of the earliest ideas of mankind, as they are reflected in Ancient Law, and to point out the relation of those ideas to modern thought. Religion/History Pages 452

Far-Away Stories *by William J. Locke* ISBN: *1-59462-129-2* **$19.45**
"Good wine needs no bush, but a collection of mixed vintages does. And this book is just such a collection. Some of the stories I do not want to remain buried for ever in the museum files of dead magazine-numbers an author's not unpardonable vanity..." Fiction Pages 272

Life of David Crockett *by David Crockett* ISBN: *1-59462-250-7* **$27.45**
"Colonel David Crockett was one of the most remarkable men of the times in which he lived. Born in humble life, but gifted with a strong will, an indomitable courage, and unremitting perseverance... Biographies/New Age Pages 424

Lip-Reading *by Edward Nitchie* ISBN: *1-59462-206-X* **$25.95**
Edward B. Nitchie, founder of the New York School for the Hard of Hearing, now the Nitchie School of Lip-Reading, Inc, wrote "LIP-READING Principles and Practice". The development and perfecting of this meritorious work on lip-reading was an undertaking... How-to Pages 400

A Handbook of Suggestive Therapeutics, Applied Hypnotism, Psychic Science ISBN: *1-59462-214-0* **$24.95**
by Henry Munro Health/New Age/Health/Self-help Pages 376

A Doll's House: and Two Other Plays *by Henrik Ibsen* ISBN: *1-59462-112-8* **$19.95**
Henrik Ibsen created this classic when in revolutionary 1848 Rome. Introducing some striking concepts in playwriting for the realist genre, this play has been studied the world over. Fiction/Classics/Plays 308

The Light of Asia *by sir Edwin Arnold* ISBN: *1-59462-204-3* **$13.95**
In this poetic masterpiece, Edwin Arnold describes the life and teachings of Buddha. The man who was to become known as Buddha to the world was born as Prince Gautama of India but he rejected the worldly riches and abandoned the reigns of power when... Religion/History/Biographies Pages 170

The Complete Works of Guy de Maupassant *by Guy de Maupassant* ISBN: *1-59462-157-8* **$16.95**
"For days and days, nights and nights, I had dreamed of that first kiss which was to consecrate our engagement, and I knew not on what spot I should put my lips..." Fiction/Classics Pages 240

The Art of Cross-Examination *by Francis L. Wellman* ISBN: *1-59462-309-0* **$26.95**
Written by a renowned trial lawyer, Wellman imparts his experience and uses case studies to explain how to use psychology to extract desired information through questioning. How-to/Science/Reference Pages 408

Answered or Unanswered? *by Louisa Vaughan* ISBN: *1-59462-248-5* **$10.95**
Miracles of Faith in China Religion Pages 112

The Edinburgh Lectures on Mental Science (1909) *by Thomas* ISBN: *1-59462-008-3* **$11.95**
This book contains the substance of a course of lectures recently given by the writer in the Queen Street Hall, Edinburgh. Its purpose is to indicate the Natural Principles governing the relation between Mental Action and Material Conditions... New Age/Psychology Pages 148

Ayesha *by H. Rider Haggard* ISBN: *1-59462-301-5* **$24.95**
Verily and indeed it is the unexpected that happens! Probably if there was one person upon the earth from whom the Editor of this, and of a certain previous history, did not expect to hear again... Classics Pages 380

Ayala's Angel *by Anthony Trollope* ISBN: *1-59462-352-X* **$29.95**
The two girls were both pretty, but Lucy who was twenty-one who supposed to be simple and comparatively unattractive, whereas Ayala was credited, as her Bombwhat romantic name might show, with poetic charm and a taste for romance. Ayala when her father died was nineteen... Fiction Pages 484

The American Commonwealth *by James Bryce* ISBN: *1-59462-286-8* **$34.45**
An interpretation of American democratic political theory. It examines political mechanics and society from the perspective of Scotsman James Bryce Politics Pages 572

Stories of the Pilgrims *by Margaret P. Pumphrey* ISBN: *1-59462-116-0* **$17.95**
This book explores pilgrims religious oppression in England as well as their escape to Holland and eventual crossing to America on the Mayflower, and their early days in New England... History Pages 268

QTY

The Fasting Cure *by Sinclair Upton*   ISBN: *1-59462-222-1*   **$13.95**

In the Cosmopolitan Magazine for May, 1910, and in the Contemporary Review (London) for April, 1910, I published an article dealing with my experiences in fasting. I have written a great many magazine articles, but never one which attracted so much attention... New Age/Self Help/Health Pages 164

☐

Hebrew Astrology *by Sepharial*   ISBN: *1-59462-308-2*   **$13.45**

In these days of advanced thinking it is a matter of common observation that we have left many of the old landmarks behind and that we are now pressing forward to greater heights and to a wider horizon than that which represented the mind-content of our progenitors...   Astrology Pages 144

☐

Thought Vibration or The Law of Attraction in the Thought World   ISBN: *1-59462-127-6*   **$12.95**

by William Walker Atkinson   Psychology/Religion Pages 144

☐

Optimism *by Helen Keller*   ISBN: *1-59462-108-X*   **$15.95**

Helen Keller was blind, deaf, and mute since 19 months old, yet famously learned how to overcome these handicaps, communicate with the world, and spread her lectures promoting optimism. An inspiring read for everyone...   Biographies/Inspirational Pages 84

☐

Sara Crewe *by Frances Burnett*   ISBN: *1-59462-360-0*   **$9.45**

In the first place, Miss Minchin lived in London. Her home was a large, dull, tall one, in a large, dull square, where all the houses were alike, and all the sparrows were alike, and where all the door-knockers made the same heavy sound...   Childrens/Classic Pages 88

☐

The Autobiography of Benjamin Franklin *by Benjamin Franklin*   ISBN: *1-59462-135-7*   **$24.95**

The Autobiography of Benjamin Franklin has probably been more extensively read than any other American historical work, and no other book of its kind has had such ups and downs of fortune. Franklin lived for many years in England, where he was agent...   Biographies/History Pages 332

☐

Name	
Email	
Telephone	
Address	
City, State ZIP	

☐ **Credit Card**   ☐ **Check / Money Order**

Credit Card Number	
Expiration Date	
Signature	

Please Mail to: Book Jungle
PO Box 2226
Champaign, IL 61825
or Fax to: 630-214-0564

ORDERING INFORMATION

web: *www.bookjungle.com*
email: *sales@bookjungle.com*
fax: *630-214-0564*
mail: *Book Jungle PO Box 2226 Champaign, IL 61825*
or PayPal *to sales@bookjungle.com*

Please contact us for bulk discounts

DIRECT-ORDER TERMS

**20% Discount if You Order
Two or More Books**
Free Domestic Shipping!
Accepted: Master Card, Visa,
Discover, American Express

www.ingramcontent.com/pod-product-compliance
Lightning Source LLC
Chambersburg PA
CBHW080908020726

47502CB00008B/2386